Marion Brunet is 43 and lives in Marseille. After university, she worked as a special-needs educator with a focus on psychiatry. Well known as a novelist in the young-adult genre, her breakthrough in literary crime fiction came with *Summer of Reckoning*, also published by Bitter Lemon Press, the winner of the 2018 Grand Prix de Littérature Policière, the prestigious French crime-fiction prize.

VANDA

Marion Brunet

Translated by Katherine Gregor

BITTER LEMON PRESS
LONDON

BITTER LEMON PRESS

First published in the United Kingdom in 2022 by
Bitter Lemon Press, 47 Wilmington Square, London WC1X 0ET

www.bitterlemonpress.com

First published in French in 2020 as *VANDA* by Editions Albin Michel, Paris
© Editions Albin Michel – Paris 2020

English translation © Katherine Gregor, 2022

A CIP record for this book is available from the British Library

ISBN 978–1–913394–653
eB USC ISBN 978–1–913394–660
eB ROW ISBN 978–1–913394–677

Bitter Lemon Press gratefully acknowledges the financial assistance of
the Arts Council of England and the Centre National du Livre.

Typeset by Tetragon Publishing Limited
Printed and bound by CPI Group (UK) Ltd, Croydon CR0 4YY

He Won't Stay

She's recognized him immediately, stopped breathing, frozen. He's having a drink next to the speakers, a restrained swaying of the head, the bored smile of a guy who hasn't hung around this sort of place for a long time.

What the hell is he doing here? Vanda hasn't seen him for almost seven years. Seven years is a long time, another lifetime – a cliché for a physical reality. The guy isn't moving, he's always been like that, it's only during sex that he'd go into motion, surprisingly unsystematic and eager.

Turning her back to the stage, Vanda walks through the group of dancers, pushes past the sweaty bodies and the jerking, colliding torsos. Glowing orange faces twist in the light, teeth exposed. As the group on the stage gets more and more excited and the mood at the bar goes up a notch, she realizes she's already a bit plastered. Dizzy from the drink and feeling invaded on her patch. He, there, next to the speakers, is no longer a part of her landscape, but superimposed like an insect on a favourite painting. She's got to go home, run away from the guy who's suddenly popped out of the woodwork – fuck, she'd better get a move on before he sees her. She slinks over to the bar and orders a vodka. Last one, she tells the barman, who smiles and doesn't believe her. He couldn't care less if she's lying – he sees worse than her every night. He also often sees her and has done for a long time. Through habit, this bar's also become a kind of pretend family, people to have a laugh with even if you don't feel like it, pissheads who become closer than the cousins you used to mess about with or your own kids. It's the only place where you can still hear punk groups play like they're smashing a bus shelter or a ticket machine. Slightly dirty rock for partying drink buddies. There are others like her here, damaged goods that forgot to grow old. Vanda downs her vodka in a large, single gulp that barely stings, and puts the glass back down on the counter brusquely.

Because she's in a rush, she keeps to her word and waves away the barman's offer as he picks up the bottle again. She seldom refuses the last drink on the house, but she really has to dash now, hasn't got time to waste, too much to lose and her hands are shaking.

There are guys smoking on the pavement – one of them motions goodbye and giggles as he staggers.

"Bye, Vanda, mind yourself on the coast road."

She doesn't reply and lights a cigarette before unlocking her ancient Renault 21 she'll never be able to afford to replace. She paid an arm and a leg to the mechanic for a new timing belt to replace the last, so now it doesn't make such a racket when she drives, such a treat. Shaking with a nervous giggle, she slides into the driver's seat. The giggle of a drunk woman or a girl sneaking out without permission. A quirky, embarrassing giggle. But just as she's about to start the engine, he's there, right next to her, so close he makes her jump – he's put a hand on the door, where the window's rolled down. He says nothing, just smiles. She can see he's aged, it suits him. As she keeps shtum, stunned, he pulls his face away, feeling awkward perhaps.

"I'm in the area for a few days. Be nice to grab a drink."

So she doesn't have to answer, she grunts, drools a *yeah* that means the opposite and starts the car. She has to leave. He won't stay.

She steps on the accelerator to drive off as fast as possible, so he has to let go of the door.

Vanda cuts across the city centre and drives alongside the sea, her head leaning towards the open window, because it feels good and for the slap of coolness that allows her to stay awake. She thinks about Simon – time to call the guy she bumped into at the bar by name, the guy from a long time ago. The mate of a mate of a mate, many of them used to hang around in a gang back then, go to all the private views so they could drink the free aperitifs and fill their pockets with peanuts. All artists, more or less, some more than others, all more or less crazy, some more than others. They had good fun. Their relationship lasted a few months, then he left and she didn't think he'd come back, she really didn't.

Grimacing in the night, Vanda tries to push the memory away and hums to herself while rolling her shoulders for an invisible audience. It's only when she takes the shortcut to the beach that she falls silent and calms down. Here, there's the sound of the waves and the animal in-breath of the backwash. She doesn't lock her car. Nobody'd want it. She always parks it in the same spot, right up against the parapet that looks down on the beach; the neighbours, those in the villas, don't say anything – she's been living here a long time, even if she's not really allowed to. There's sand stuck on the radiator grille and in the grooves of the practically smooth tyres. There's also sand everywhere inside, under her buttocks and on the floor, a bloody mess in the rear, seats tilted back. Tins of paint, turpentine, white spirit, bits of wood and a plastic spade. And the unrolled sleeping bag with a hump.

At the noise of the hatch opening, something stirs in the sleeping bag. The child wakes up, but not completely, just enough to extricate himself from the bag and cling to his mother, who lifts him onto her hip and half carries him – he doesn't weigh much, even though he's six. In her state, going down the steps to the hut is an acrobatic feat, but she's used to it because she often takes him along and comes back home with him at night. But it's harder on the sand, so she almost collapses and her foot knocks against an abandoned beer can. It makes her snigger feebly, though she doesn't feel quite as drunk any more – it's the road, the wind, and now the smell of the sea and its motion. And the child's body, his head rolling against her.

As gently as she can, she opens the thin shutter, then the door, and closes it behind them and on the only room, unable to see anything. She takes the child to the large bed, he slinks under the duvet, an arm over the sheet, and immediately falls back to sleep, his mouth half open, his temples still moist with night sweat. Vanda crouches next to him, sinks her face into his neck to smell him, his night scents. She devours him with kisses at the risk of waking him again.

"My baby, my Limpet, I love you, I love you."

A litany, a gentle, demented song – her boy is fast asleep and doesn't wake up.

Limpet

"Mummy, come back!" the child yells at the waves.

Vanda's guessing that he put on his red anorak and wrapped a scarf around his neck before coming out on the beach. A little spot wriggling on the sand. It's a bitter January cold and the sea is glassy, but runs deep. Vanda dives again and braces her body for another breaststroke in the icy water. She's gone for a swim, as she often does all year round. Especially on hangover mornings. She avoids very windy days, when the waves get bad, even in the Mediterranean. The water sometimes comes all the way up to the door of the hut and you have to be clever to reach the steps. As a matter of fact, they sometimes get stuck indoors because of it, and then the house becomes a cage for Vanda and a boat or a pirate hideaway for the child. Limpet loves getting stuck with his mother. Limpet's not his real name, of course, he's really Noé, but Limpet has stuck since he was tiny. He doesn't know if he likes his nickname, doesn't really question it. If his mother uses it, then it must be all right. But there's also the fact a friend of Vanda's told him about the limpets that eat drowned people's eyes. When he heard that, he naturally pictured swollen, white bodies, eyes open to the sky or turned towards the seabed, and the little shells munching at their eyeballs. Sometimes, he has nightmares about it.

Noé is fidgeting outside the hut, grimacing and making noises with his mouth for reassurance and to erase the distance. Vanda's an excellent swimmer but the sea is so deep, and her pin-sized head above the water makes something hurt in the middle of his tummy, a vague anxiety that bites him harder when the sky is grey.

She's heard his cry and dives back under. She feels her mass of hair pull her head back and stick to her neck when she emerges. The blood's flowing better in her body and the cold gives her a boost of energy. Salt water goes up her nostrils and she coughs on the surface, spits in the light. Where she is, the bottom has vanished. She sometimes imagines things beneath, real things like moray eels with chiselled teeth or stuff that doesn't exist – vengeful drowned people who could grab her ankle, underwater monsters or film sharks. There are only catsharks here, but great whites have been seen close to Mediterranean coasts, in Mahdia, Tangier and even the Balearic Islands. So why not here?

She feels guilty about earlier. When they woke up, the child tried to make her some coffee, using the bottle from the mineral water cut in half, and a filter made of toilet paper. They have an electric coffee maker, but it doesn't work any more and Vanda keeps saying she's going to buy another one, except that she remembers only when she wants a coffee. Then she forgets. He heated the water on the gas stove. He's good at it – he's a careful, observant kid. He likes the smell of coffee and to suck his mother's teaspoon, scrape the sugar from the bottom of the cup.

When she gets up before him or if she comes back before he's awake, the smell of coffee's like a caress.

The child poured the boiling water into the bottle amazingly delicately and patiently for a child of six. Only, the weight of the liquid toppled the bottle, some of the filtered coffee spilled on the floor, all over the place, on the fridge, the armchair and even his sweater, and that suddenly made her lose her temper. She slapped him, called him an idiot and even a little shit.

"You're not the one who has to clean it up. Damn it, I've had it up to here with your nonsense."

She was clenching her teeth.

The little boy had placed around the gas stove figurines he likes, plastic Pokémon and realistic animals, dinosaurs and two dragons. The bottle was almost full, the coffee was dark.

As she insulted him, Vanda, dishevelled, punched the soft mattress. She suddenly got up and swept the animals off with the back of her hand. Then she started to cry, sobbing like a lost puppy, took him in her arms and held him too tight.

"My baby, my darling, forgive me, my Limpet, forgive me, forgive me."

She hates it when she does this. It's so overwhelming and afterwards she wants to die or rewind or learn to keep her mouth shut and be a gentle mother like the others. She went swimming.

Noé's lived in the hut since he was born, it's his home. Some people tell Vanda she should leave. That she and Noé could move into an apartment in the city centre, higher up and with light flooding the floor tiles, curtains at the windows and a room each. Also a washing machine; that would be useful. At the moment, she has to sneak around at work and do their washing in the laundrette. Vanda always shakes her head and says *no, this is our home* and *besides, there's the sea.* She does think about it sometimes, when it's cold despite the oil heater and the kid's doing his homework in his anorak, or if she brings a guy home. *I can't afford it anyway,* she says. *It's less expensive than a two-bed in the city centre. And besides, there's the sea.*

It's Sunday, so no school, and his mother's going to drag her feet all day. Noé smiles. He's a bit tense because she's taking her time coming back, but he loves Sundays with no constraints. What they find difficult on Sundays is that people come to the beach, even if they don't swim. There's some on other days, too, but they're not so much in the way.

Slowly, Noé repeats the procedure, boils the water and filters it into the bottle. This time, he doesn't spill anything. He puts the pan on the worktop and decants the coffee into the flask, screws the top back on and takes it outside the hut with him, holding it tight against his stomach. She sees him sitting on the concrete step between the beach and the hut, his eyes searching the horizon and finding her. She's nearer now, swimming to the shore with powerful strokes, towards him, and that gives her a feeling of warmth swirling in her belly. Vanda wishes she could erase her shouting from earlier, and her vile words. She stares at the little red dot that grows as she gets closer to the shore and swims faster, harder. All it takes is a little distance for her to want to go back to him so desperately it hurts.

Hangover

He recognized her straight away, as soon as she walked into the bar. He even wonders if he didn't pick that very place in the hope of bumping into her. And yet he'd sworn to himself he wouldn't try and see her. She's a nutcase, is what he'd told himself, how could I have fallen in love with such a nutcase, but deep down he knew it hadn't just been about her but about them, about the times, and that's what they liked about it – the fact that they weren't like the others, that they went down to the wire. Still, he felt weird seeing her again, she hasn't changed much – or rather she has, but he doesn't realize it. Glued to the speakers, drowning in the noise, he remembered odds and ends: her broad laughter, excessive and exhilarating to the point of causing embarrassment; her breasts, always perky, with their pink halos; her tattoos, which he'd trace with his fingertips; her indifference. Simon wasn't sure he wanted to renew his contact with her. Too borderline for him, too insane – Simon likes reassuring things, unambiguous laughter, and he observes the speed limit. After she left the bar, he breathed more easily and drained his glass in a single gulp. But then seeing her closer, talking to her. Her presence did make him feel uncomfortable and he hates this weakness of his. Afterwards, he stood on the pavement, upset, the wind in his face – he'd forgotten how these gusts can drive you insane. He had a lot to drink, bumped into an old pal and drank some more.

This morning his head's about to explode. His tongue's so dry it's like it doesn't belong to him. He staggers to the kitchen and drinks from the tap, his head cocked in the sink, until he's breathless.

Simon hasn't been back here for seven years and these few days are like a self-commemoration. He's not here just for the sake of it – he wouldn't have come back, of course, if his mother hadn't died.

The bars are still the same and in every place, he sees himself as he was seven years ago. *Seven years ago*: it gives one gravitas and the status of a mature man. It's a lot and something of a landmark, it means a guy who's lived. *I haven't been here for seven years*, he's been thinking for two days, every time he comes across a bistro, a street or a square, or a place where memories catch up with him, like a mate from his previous life. And, soon, it makes him feel like he's simply grown older.

He opens the fridge and takes out a piece of ham which he stuffs into his mouth, hardly chewing it, the kind of thing you do when you're on your own.

His head feels heavy, his eyes bloated. He should go back to bed but doesn't want to sacrifice the sunlight hours to another coma. Still, what he really needs is someone to stroke his neck and take care of him. He grabs his mobile and goes back to bed with it.

Chloé answers at the second ring – the phone must be grafted to her hand. "Just woken up?"

Her voice is amused, or perhaps concerned. Simon almost smiles, tells her about the night, the booze and the old pal. He's already feeling guilty. Simon always feels guilty and Chloé triggers that in him even more, even if she doesn't do it on purpose. It was the same with his mother. And now he's wondering if it was right to go out after his mother's just died, so shame comes on top of guilt.

"Did you see her?"

"Yes."

"Was it tough?"

He hesitates, finding the question idiotic but at the same time considerate. He wonders why he called her.

"It's not exactly fun. But the nurses got her dressed. My aunt chose the clothes."

"I'm sorry I'm not there."

"Never mind. You'll be here for the funeral. I think that's better, actually. I'm going to have to put up with my family and that's going to be bloody awful."

"Honestly, if I'd been able to take time off work—"

"Chloé, it really doesn't matter."

Chloé sighs. He wants to cut the conversation short and mentions a shower and a cousin to see. When they hang up, Simon buries his head in a pillow, moaning. Images of his mother in the hospital bed take over and remind him that he wasn't there.

Simon looks for excuses: his life, the distance, that son-of-a-bitch stepfather of his. He sinks deeper under the duvet with violet gentian patterns. He's gone for the sofa bed in the lounge: no way is he sleeping in the bed where his mother and stepfather treated themselves to a new life. He'd sooner drop dead.

He doesn't know if his own life is the first or is unique or one of a multitude. He's from a different era than the old folks even though he's getting on, given his wrinkles and the white hairs in his three-day-old beard. He thinks he's free because he still enjoys rock 'n' roll, fancies himself daring because he's self-employed. As for his insincerity, his averting his eyes so he doesn't get bogged down with problem-solving and untying knots, that's something he's not aware of. He finds it hard to be alive and make choices. He's aged so fast, the speed of it is unfair. In his mind he has no white hairs. He's a bit of a coward and mildly unhappy. A starchy, almost aesthetic unhappiness. His mother's just died, so he tells himself he's got an excuse. He's not sure he wants Chloé to join him. But he's incapable of telling her.

On the wall, there are pictures of him from over the years, not everywhere but, still, there are quite a few of them. It's fun to see himself as a kid, holding his mother's arm, she's so feminine in her A-line dress. When he saw her at the hospital, she was so grey and so dried up. It's true that she didn't often visit him. You'd think she preferred him in photos. Simon swallows this small bitterness with some spite – he didn't often visit either, that is, never. Even for Christmas, they'd tend to gather at his uncle's in the Cévennes. He couldn't bear family Christmases. Now he'll no longer be obliged to go, he wonders if he's going to miss them.

In another photo, he's almost an adult and smiling at the camera. It's either the day he passed his Baccalauréat or a birthday, he can't remember. His downturned eyes give him a meek expression despite the fire driving him in this late adolescence he remembers well.

The apartment is his now, so he'll have to empty it. He's thinking of selling it, that would be better. He doesn't want to live here any more anyway. Here, it's his previous life. Maybe, after all, he's had several lives.

Next Time

And yet she'd promised herself it wouldn't happen again. Only, it always does. She came straight from the psychiatric ward to the school, but it took ages to find a spot because the traffic warden wouldn't let her double-park. She wanted to tell him where to get off, but kept it in and refrained from showing the stubborn bastard the finger. She's making progress. When she arrives at the gates, out of breath, Noé is all alone, or almost: a teacher is holding him by the hand. Her expression leaves nothing to the imagination: it's brimming with anxiety and anger – and you can see contempt just beneath.

"I had trouble parking."

The teacher doesn't answer. She has a red fringe cut straight across her forehead and Vanda can see that under her multicoloured dress she's freezing her arse off. The woollen cardigan she's pulling tighter over her doesn't seem enough. Vanda thinks she looks like an advert for eco-conscious jam. Noé rushes to bury himself in his mother's body, arms open: there's no resentment in him. He gently tugs at her arm to let her know he wants to go, that he wants to get away from school as soon as possible. But the young woman gives Vanda a look that holds her back.

"I must speak to you. These delays can't go on. And I haven't seen anything in the book about his absence last week."

"Excuse me?"

"The parent–teacher contact book. You have to justify Noé's absences, you know that?"

Vanda squints under the weight of the reproach. Everything inside her rebels against this humiliation, this tone of voice, and the abyss the young woman is digging between them. Noé squeezes his mother's hand. They're allies, that's nice. She decides to smile thanks to the cool pressure of his little fingers.

"Yes, I'll remember next time."

"It's not enough to remember, this mustn't happen again. And I can't stay an extra twenty minutes with Noé every evening. Surely, you can make arrangements with another mum, can't you?"

Vanda doesn't feel like making any more effort. She thinks of Magalie, with her Coke and her cigarette, in the garden of the hospital. She suddenly envies her right to insult people without consequences. It would be great to tell the teacher to shut her mouth, but not a clever move. So Vanda doesn't respond, leaves without a word and walks off with Noé at the end of her arm. But, behind her, the teacher doesn't relent. She had trouble starting, but now she won't stop.

"I know it's hard for you and that you and Noé live on the beach, but I'm warning you, next time I'll have to inform social services."

Vanda closes her eyes, clasps her son's hand hard and picks up the pace.

"Right, you do that, bitch."

She doesn't say it loud enough for the teacher to hear her, but almost.

There are people on the beach when they get there. Not tourists, no, but mates. Ten or so of them, with packs of beer, cheering them as they arrive.

"Vanda, we've been waiting for you!"

"Hi, kid."

"Hi, Limpet."

"Hi, Noé."

The child smiles and runs to the door of the hut. He doesn't like kissing people, except his mother. He says hello, waves and waits for Vanda to open the door so he can dive home. Impromptu drink parties with mates take place on the beach even in the winter. In any case, spring's on the way. Vanda doesn't let the gang into their den. It's too small and, besides, it's their lair. But it allows her to put the beer in the fridge and switch on the loudspeakers. And the girls can at least pee indoors. The guys go to the rocks or the water's edge. Sometimes, one of them stays behind after the others have gone: that one's allowed in but, with a kid, it's complicated.

Jimmy's trying to roll a joint under his jacket. It's tricky in the wind, he hurls insults at every gust and that makes the others laugh. Vanda fetches a blanket and puts it over his shoulders, so Jimmy can have a shelter to roll his joint more easily and because it's cold this evening. When she plays the Pixies a bit loud to drown out the wind and the waves, they all give a happy groan as they recognize the opening chords. They stand still and love it. Later, she'll play The Clash. Or Bowie. Or Rammstein. Classics that warm them up and make them nod in time with the music. Jimmy lights the joint and takes the first drag with glee. His name isn't really Jimmy, of course, and he isn't American. No one remembers how this nickname started, not even him. The joint circulates and the fat smoke flies away with bits of burning ash. Everyone shields their eyes with their hands, fingers curled around their bottles. They talk about the roadworks on Jean-Jaurès and about the millions spent on gentrifying the La Plaine area. They consider action, something to screw things up and scare the security men guarding the building site. Isabelle sighs, says they're too old for that, and tells them they're threatening to take her unemployment allowance from her, because she declined a job offer as a warehouse worker as she's a visual artist; Sam gets all het up about his casual work and the fact he hasn't clocked in enough days this month. It's stressful for everybody except Fred, who teaches computing classes at the recently opened institute and even landed a real contract. Vanda doesn't really know them. They're straight out of a student past that's been drifting further and further away every year, or out of the various drinking sessions that stud their lives. They're losers and she shares some of their marginality, which has become the norm around her, what with the general decline. But she's always kept her distance, maintained the small screen that needs to melt away before mates can become friends. She's not good at that.

Noé emerges from the hut with a handful of dinosaurs. Without looking at anyone, he places them facing the sea, their legs firmly in the sand, calls his mother so she can come and see, explains the conflicts between the various species and whispers the names of some of them. She loves it but isn't listening to a word. All she cares about is Noé's focused little face, her world.

Vanda has a lot of recollections from her own childhood that she doesn't tell anyone about. She's one of those people you think were born adults, just as they are now, even if they're immature. She has palpable flaws, evident vulnerability, but she gives away very little. They know she arrived here just over ten years ago and some of them met her back then. Before that, it's a blank. She immersed herself in the city until she became a part of it, as though devoid of any past. And now she belongs here. From the white cliffs of Les Goudes to the bars on Cours Julien, shopkeepers, bar owners and greengrocers all know this woman with big, curly hair, who speaks little, and her kid, who's growing up fast. Many know she lives in a hut and that's unusual. No one says anything, but it's probably against the law, even if there's drinking water. Here, what's unlawful is a movable feast and sometimes gives way to what's legitimate, just because it's been done that way for so long. At first, the area's old folks eyed her with suspicion, but then she blended into the surroundings.

Even if she doesn't talk about it, Vanda lived in Brittany until she was twenty. She's familiar with changing skies, the sublime greyness of thunderstorms, the silver at the edge of the forest, the liquid clouds, and all the shades before and after the rain. She's also familiar with waterlogged paths and soft, sticky mud, because she lived in a village inland and not on the coast. She finds the blue here unchangeable and full, reassuring. It pushes doubt away and wards off destruction. In fact, it's a blue that wards off the end of the world. When Vanda left Brittany, after getting her Baccalauréat at resits by the skin of her teeth and two years late, she started art school but didn't even last a year. She stayed just long enough to meet the most rebellious in her class, the most daring, the party animals. She quickly realized she was in the wrong place, even though she didn't know why, exactly. Back then, she felt she didn't belong to that world, and this was proved by a too-realistic painting she proudly presented during her first term, and which was received with restrained sniggers and condescending looks. She felt lost and humiliated. So she borrowed a language that belonged to others in order to get by without too much emotional damage, ideas about art and teaching that she found obsolete and ridiculous. Odd jobs, cleaning and serving in bars and restaurants, felt more reassuring, and at least that way she could earn some money. Her contract at the psychiatric hospital, renewed every three months for the past two years, is a blessing.

After leaving art school, Vanda carried on drawing but just for herself and decided to stay here, in the light of the monochrome skies. The others, standing there, smoking, giggling and passing around another joint, blotted their copybooks in other ways. No better, sometimes worse. She's been hanging around these success rejects, these losers, for a long time. They socialize with her and don't ask questions any more.

In the fading light, Noé's face is orange and his eyes golden. Vanda sits behind him and hugs him. She now wishes the others would go away. Even Jimmy, who's smiling at her as if trying to say he'd quite like to stay a little longer. As a matter of fact, he comes up and leans over her.

"I can go and buy some pizzas, if you like."

"No, we're going to spend the evening together, just the two of us. I'm not throwing you all out, but Noé has to go to bed early and I'm also exhausted."

Jimmy looks disappointed. He toys with the sand, grabs it by the handful and lets it run between his fingers, then does it again.

"I forgot to tell you Simon's in the area."

"I know."

"He'd like to see you again, at least that's what he said. We were drunk out of our skulls but he hasn't really changed. He doesn't look like he's angry with you any more, but then there's also been a lot of water under the bridge."

"Why would he be angry with me?"

"No, that's right, I don't know, maybe because you dumped him and stuff."

Vanda lifts her head and looks at Jimmy. She's annoyed and worried, you can tell by the way her pupils have shrunk and the furrow between her eyebrows has got deeper. Also, her neck stretches aristocratically, like a cobra.

"So?"

"No, nothing, never mind, I just wanted to tell you he wants to see you. His mother died, that's why he's back. Call him, I'll text you his new number."

*

After the mates leave, Vanda and Noé stay rooted in the sand a little longer, like the dinosaurs' paws. They watch the sun sink into the water, Vanda keeps her arms tight around the child. She feels anxiety rise, like a black wave about to come crashing over them. She knows the fact he's back and insisting he wants to see her again are signs. It's like a squall, the colour of the sky changing before a storm. Her son's body reassures her: it's a palpable reality, it's the best she has. The two of them, all alone. Nothing but her son and her, that's all that matters in the final analysis. Her face against the back of his neck, she sniffs his scent like an animal and refrains from biting him.

"I'd die for you."

The child stiffens and wishes he could escape her embrace.

"What's on the other side?"

"I've already told you. If you swim straight ahead, you get to Algeria. If you drift to the side, it's Morocco."

"Are we going to go there?"

"Yes, my love, we'll go."

Tangier

To cross the Mediterranean on a boat and land in Tangier had been a certainty hatched on a drunken evening a few weeks after the break-up. Simon had left town and she'd already forgotten him. Tangier had been a revelation, a beam of pure light through the clouds. Tangier sounded as powerful as a poem, as a promise. Perhaps she hoped that her dream of creativity wasn't dead and would be reborn there. The city was home to a history that included artists who'd got stuck there, the twentieth-century damned ones, the splendid junkies. On the rooftops of the kasbah, she'd dreamed of exile as others had done before her, and her notepads were filled with sketches and splashes of words. In the end, she had smoked some fat, generous weed that left her panting with laughter and emotions, day after day, for two months, until a particular event that was to change her life. At first, she'd hung around cafés, slept on the guest house roof despite the chant of the muezzin, met expats and Tangierians, and listened to stories. She'd found a rhythm and a way of being. But no poem or drawing that was up to scratch. She lacked the spark or else the willpower – or perhaps the need. And yet nothing had escaped her, from the light emerging above the rooftops to the cries of the animals – goats, cockerels or starving roaming cats. The scents, the sounds and especially the slowness. And the blue. As she looked at Tangier harbour from the square with the cannons, she figured nothing, nothing at all, could alter this blue. She felt it but couldn't utter it. She could have stayed and lived there for years, especially since the cost of living was lower than in France. Even so, had she had to roam around on her own, on her savings alone, things would have been different. But she'd been lucky to meet Joseph and Françoise. Someone in the harbour had told her about this elderly French couple, sailors who'd stopped over there and never left, and who welcomed destitute young people into their home, whether they were locals or newcomers. She toyed with the idea of going to meet them, since the guest house where she'd put down her bag was eating away at her savings and she wanted to stay.

A guy had pointed at the terrace of a café, in the shade of a bramble bush: *Joseph is the one with the Caisse d'Épargne T-shirt*. She'd thought that odd, an adventurer who wears a T-shirt with the logo of a bank. Later, he told her how, twenty years earlier, he'd quit after six months, unable to bear the abyss between his job and life in the broad sense of the word. The T-shirt was a reminder, thumbing your nose, an old joke. As for Françoise, her overly bright dresses competed with the hibiscus. Taller and wider than her husband, her speech and her body took up a space their adopted country struggled to grant her. Why they'd chosen Tangier after years of sailing, Vanda never found out. It never even occurred to her to ask them, and that was proof that this city was like an anchor, the land furrowed with dry wrinkles, and the blue – both sky and sea – as smooth as a child's cheek. You could choose to either be born again or grow old there, which is actually the same thing.

Joseph and Françoise housed and fed her. She listened to their stories, about the damage suffered off the coast of Cape Verde, the route of the trade winds, Brazil, as well as the Mediterranean, livelier and more dangerous than you'd think. Françoise spoke warmly about their friends aboard other sailboats, who, like them, travelled across the oceans between the continents, those who were still there, those who became sedentary again, and those who'd been shipwrecked. Since the internet, she'd got into the habit of receiving and giving news, even to those she'd only met once, even if they'd just shared a meal, a bottle, or a piece of advice about how to get a reef in safely in the middle of a storm.

Vanda would listen, fascinated by these lives led outside the world, comforted by the solidity under her feet. Since Tangier and Françoise's stories, she's been more aware of the ground under her heels – soil, rock, asphalt or sand – even if she still swims in the open sea. Françoise enjoyed talking about their years of sailing, but was happy not to travel any more. Vanda guessed by the way she touched objects, took possession of spaces, and by her obvious relief at being able to spread out after years in a tiny saloon at sea. Joseph, on the other hand, pretended he believed they'd set off again soon. Vanda never knew if he really meant it or if it was his way of not ageing.

Françoise never contradicted him whenever he talked of a new departure. She would defer to him then smile at her lodgers and reassure them: it wouldn't happen tomorrow, so they could sleep soundly.

During the weeks Vanda spent at their house, five other lodgers moved in. They all slept in the living room with the flower-patterned banquettes or else on the rooftop terrace covered in rugs bleached by the sun. One evening, Françoise played a Wanda Jackson record hoping she'd like it, but it upset her. The crackling rockabilly obviously reminded her of her mother. Joseph and Françoise embarked on an energetic rock 'n' roll dance and were quickly out of breath, especially as they couldn't stop laughing. The music was flying over the city and Vanda thought it must be entering every riad, every kasbah apartment, through every window. Her temples were throbbing as she thought again about her mother, in this place, among people who came closest to what she hoped for in a family. She pictured her mother twisting in the kitchen to this outmoded rock, eyes always moist at the more languid country music. She'd try to get her to dance but Vanda had stopped finding that fun after the age of twelve. She'd disappear to her room and leave her mother twirling on her own to Lee Moses, Wanda Jackson, Dolly Parton or the great Elvis. Her first name was slightly different to that of the rockabilly singer only because the clerk at the town hall had refused to spell it with a *w*, considering it too American. Her mother insisted but he wouldn't budge. Vanda knows the story, as well as the music of the woman she's named after. Françoise dragged her out of her recollection by trying to get her to dance, too, but she smiled apologetically, suppressing the insidious nostalgia that had just slapped her across the face. She rolled a joint, focusing on every move, precise and absent.

A few days later, as she left Cinéma Rif and was walking across Petit Socco to go into the medina, something happened. She'd just been to see *Gloria* again and was smiling at the thought of young Tangierians taking advantage of the darkness to kiss, arranging to meet in the dark without seeing anything of Gena Rowlands's beauty. As she walked past the vegetable stalls, the smell of coriander made her nauseous. It was so radical, so violent that she knew straight away.

Oddly, she didn't think of Simon but only about this other creature that had lodged inside her in order to grow. Standing motionless in the crowd, suddenly blind and deaf, she turned inwards to quiz this new presence. It was there, alive, totally alien and mind-blowingly intimate.

Tangier killed off her last dreams as an artist and greeted the upheaval of a life.

She had to leave and remember that Tangier was a stopover. Social security, French hospitals, even if packed, weren't to be sneezed at. Joseph and Françoise encouraged her to go back and invited her to return later. No doubt they'd still be there.

She plans to go back there someday and take Noé with her. Unless it's the prospect alone that reassures her, like a folded life jacket you keep at the bottom of a boat taking on water.

Are You Coming Back?

Simon's stacking his mother's clothes into cardboard boxes. He doesn't recognize half of them and it's like he's folding the laundry of a stranger. He feels even more like an intruder when he empties her underwear drawer. The lace feels heavy in his large, man's hands and it makes him want to cry. He sits on the edge of the bed, pieces of silky fabric crumpled in his clenched fists.

As he was growing up, Simon felt the shift: it wasn't him fleeing his mother but the other way around. She had been left alone with him until his teenage years, and her constant sacrifice was crystal clear. She was there for him and always would be. Even if he'd suffered the absence of his father, he also knew that the latter's premature departure gave them the opportunity of a life for just the two of them, as well as this unbounded love, his mother's attention to his slightest move. He realized soon enough that it was lovely and not something to share. So when their quiet life for two capsized, Simon had a very hard time of it.

He knows now that his stepfather was no worse than any other and that he made his mother happy. That he did better than Simon's own father, who vanished shortly after he was born. Maybe he should have told this to his mother earlier, because it's too late now. But his step-father's arrival sealed the end of his childhood, so he never ceased to resent him for it. Shit, it's time he grew up – he's almost old.

What's eating him, the mass of bile that bites at his stomach, is that she'll never meet his children when he has them. Even if Chloé doesn't want to have any at the moment, she might change her mind and then what's he going to tell his kids when they ask who their grand-mother is?

When the doorbell rings, Simon jumps, almost embarrassed, and throws the underwear into a box before dragging himself reluctantly to the front door. He doesn't want to talk to anybody.

When he discovers his aunt on the doorstep, he slouches and sinks his hands into his pockets, like a teenager. She hugs him and he lets her in without really returning her embrace. It's not that he doesn't want to, he just doesn't know how, it's been such a long time.

"You're very pale."

So predictable.

"Yeah. Paris isn't exactly Marrakesh."

"You could come here more often."

"You mean I could have come here more often?"

"No need to jump down my throat just because you're upset. I'm upset too, but I'm not here shouting at you."

Simon feels like an idiot and helps his aunt remove her coat. Under the thick layer, his aunt is as round as a barrel. Her tanned, wrinkled cleavage has lost all its allure but none of its pride.

"Sorry."

"Never mind, we're all in a bit of a shock."

He goes to the kitchen to make them two coffees and raises his voice so it travels the distance between them.

"Were you with her?"

By the time he returns with the two cups, his aunt's eyes are moist. She hasn't moved or replied. She sinks on the sofa, her thighs pressed together.

"I went to see her the day before."

"You couldn't be expected to be there all the time, to be fair."

The aunt's sniffles coincide with Simon's thoughts. Her voice drops to a whisper. "She was all alone."

"We're always all alone in the end, anyway."

The aunt gives a painful little hiccup, pretends she hasn't heard.

"She missed Georges terribly."

That's it, Simon's eyes glaze over, he wants his aunt and her snivelling to go away. He feels like a shit for thinking that, but he's had enough and wants to be alone. He stares into his coffee, focuses on the froth and the thud of the cup on the wooden table. On top of everything else, she must have had to take the bus, she lives in Catalans, fuck, as long as she doesn't stay for the whole day, he really doesn't need that. He wonders if it's because she mentioned Georges that he suddenly wants her to leave, tells himself that's not why, because his stepfather, well, that was a long time ago, and he's dead and buried now. The aunt talks about vaults, about plots in the cemetery and grey, white or pink granite for the headstone. In any case, his mother wanted to be buried with Georges, and there's already a tombstone, so all you have to do is add her name in gold lettering. He reckons he really should thank his stepfather because, without him, it's debts he would have inherited and not a three-room apartment in Cinq-Avenues. Well, maybe not debts, his mother was careful with money, but there wasn't much money to be careful with, just about enough to pay for part of his studies. He can't for the world remember the colour of the granite, and yet he did go to his stepfather's funeral, travelled here and back to support his inconsolable mother who kept tripping along the avenues of the Saint-Pierre cemetery. She was frail all of a sudden, and that made him angry.

The aunt smells of dog: she's always had one even though her apartment isn't very large. Simon hasn't set foot there for years, but remembers it. He used to go and swim in Catalans when he was a child. The aunt would give him and his cousin a set of keys, and they'd sometimes come in for a bite to eat or to have a shower to soothe their scorched skin. He remembers the taste of salt on his lips, chapped on the edges from too much swimming. They'd raid the fridge, leave crumbs and ham grease on the oilcloth before going back to dive between the large boulders. It's all so far away and yet so near.

"Is Christelle all right?"

"How should I know? Do you hear from her?"

The aunt grumbles but this familiar lament looks like an act. Simon smiles, finding his aunt's bad mood more reassuring than her tears.

"No, not for a long time."

"Exactly, I haven't either. She married an idiot, had children a long way away from her mother, and that's the

result. The little ones barely know their grandmother."
She covers her mouth with a hand and rolls her eyes.
"Sorry, my love, it's not appropriate to say this to you
now."

"I don't have children."

"But you will, and I'll be here, you know that."

She suddenly lights up at the prospect of having a
second chance, since she didn't get one with her own
daughter.

"Are you coming back?"

Simon bursts out laughing.

"No way."

"Why not? Weren't you happy here?"

He smiles without replying. Of course he was happy
here, but he had to leave, it's just the way it is, there
comes a time when if you stay you congeal, you die from
the inside. Besides, he longed for great things, for movement. He wanted to be where things are happening. The
image of a thick mane of hair in his hands, a break-up
that prompted him to escape, shift, change perspective.

He thinks about Catalans, later, about when he'd take
Vanda on his scooter to swim there. Actually, his old
scooter must still be in the garage. She'd only just moved
here, so he'd shown her around; she marvelled at seeing
the sea every day and tattoos kept sprouting on her. Her
childhood village, which she hardly ever mentioned, was
overshadowed by her enthusiasm at discovering a new
world. Since she agreed to have a drink with him, he can't
stop thinking about her. It scares the hell out of him, he
doesn't know what to expect from the meeting. Simon
turns to his aunt.

"About the funeral, the day after tomorrow, shall we meet outside Saint-Pierre? Is there a do afterwards?"

"If there's a do afterwards, it's up to you to organize it, my love. And what are you doing about the ceremony?"

A hot flush suddenly rises to his face and his fingers start tingling. His aunt clearly sees his stupor.

"Simon… you're thirty-five. Sorry to be so blunt, but it's your mother who's just died. It's up to you to take care of all this. I'm happy to help, but you're the one who has to make the decisions."

At this point, Simon realizes that things have shifted, and more than he'd wanted. Even from a distance, his mother had let him be a child and he can't remain one any more now she's dead. He finds that hard to take.

A Nutter Like Them

When she comes to work, there's a stench of shit and cleaning products. By the end of the day, she gets used to it and can't smell anything, but that initial gulp of putrid air and detergent says it all about the place. She's first welcomed by Jared and his excessive joy, his yelps and his caresses. He's always wanting to cling to you, and his overly long arms wrap around the members of staff he likes. Vanda pictures a giant octopus. And, on top of everything else, Jared drools.

"Get off, Jared, you're too revolting."

The patient giggles and sinks his fingers into Vanda's hair. Because of the night before, she has a little trouble disengaging herself and gently pushes Jared away, so he sprints down the corridor in a zigzag. Whenever his mother comes to visit, he sits on her lap and slobbers all over her breasts. The output is even more generous when he's happy or excited. Jared is forty years old but looks sixty. When he climbs on his mother to nestle against her large bosom, they look like a monstrous couple, a terrifying sculpture at the gates of hell. It's what Vanda thinks, though she doesn't say it. When Jared's mother leaves, she's always tight-lipped and has tears in the corners of her eyes. She gives him chocolates and tells him not to eat them all at once. Jared runs back to his room, screaming, like a seagull over a shoal of fish, and gobbles them all in one go. Then his drool gets all brown and his clothes damp. The laundry women sulk. He hides the box in the most improbable places, and sometimes even blocks the toilets, trying to make it disappear. As she leaves, Jared's mother sweats, glances around like a mouse in a panic and says *He's nice, really, he's a good boy. Maybe his father will come with me next week.* Except that in the twenty years Jared's been committed, he's never been here.

Vanda walks into the windowless room where the cleaners change and swaps her clothes for a baby-blue outfit, which isn't the same as that of the nurses or their aides. It wouldn't do to get the roles mixed up. Here, the only ones who wear their normal clothes – suits, jeans, jackets, shirts, English shoes or trainers – are the doctors.

You can tell by the locker doors who's got a permanent contract, and who hasn't. The lockers covered in pictures belong to the women who are going to stay. Those with provisional contracts don't risk making a mark on the place with stickers and postcards. Vanda's locker is immaculate, a bit dented and doesn't actually close. She doesn't care. There's a lot of screaming and shouting at work but thefts are rare. Besides, everyone knows cleaners aren't exactly rolling in it.

The fluorescent light attacks her, and so does the smell of bleach: it's worse than changing rooms at a swimming pool. She hated going swimming with the school when she was a teenager. She remembers two bastards in year nine teasing her because nobody'd told her she was supposed to shave her legs. Her mother certainly wouldn't have given her that kind of advice: she was too busy yielding to her lovers, hoping one of them would stick around and marry her despite that millstone daughter of hers. The two arseholes had mimicked a monkey and some girls had sniggered. And yet she was already attractive by then, but middle school leaves little room for beauty. Rather, it chooses hostility and casting stones, order and rank. It's the time of gang stupidity raised to the status of courage. She's hated swimming pools ever since.

She doesn't linger in the changing room and goes to the first ward in her pale-blue outfit, clips her thick hair on the top of her head with a plastic peg. As she's arming herself with the necessary equipment to tackle the cleaning, Samia, breathless, darts out of one of the rooms.

"Oh, great, you're here. It's better if it's two of us doing Magalie's room."

Samia must be about forty but looks ten years older, and looks even worse in the work smock, which wouldn't do even the prettiest figure any favours. She massages her back with both hands and grimaces. Her ringed fingers tense up on her lower back.

"Are you still in as much pain?"

"Worse."

Vanda sighs and shakes her head.

"You should get them to sign you off."

"I can't. If they sign me off they won't take me back."

A short-term contract, renewed every three months. Vanda knows the tune.

"Animals."

"We're the animals."

"They're not allowed to do this."

With a carnivorous, pained smile, Samia finally straightens up.

"Fuck being allowed."

"Thierry says he could give us a few tips to pressure them."

"Thierry? I don't trust trade unions."

"He's also told me something worrying, the hospital being put under supervision."

"They want to cut corners."

"Yeah… and the last ones in are the first ones out."

Samia and Vanda walk into Magalie's room. It's empty.

"Where is she?"

"In the garden. They sent her out of her room because she got out of control again."

"What did she do?"

"She didn't want to take her meds last night, so they gave her an injection by force."

"Shit."

"What's shitty is that she got her own back, and it's now down to us…"

With a gesture, Samia shows Vanda the carnage: there's blood everywhere, on the sheets and smeared on the walls, the bed frame and the light switches.

"Did she slash her wrists or what?"

"No, she didn't need to."

When Vanda understands, she feels a therapeutic laugh rise in her and is unable to restrain it.

"You find this funny, do you?"

"Sorry, it's a nervous laugh."

Samia grumbles in disapproval and puts on her latex gloves. She pours cupfuls of antiseptic detergent into a bucket of scalding water, the smell is overpowering.

"They're all nutters."

"That's why they're here."

"Aren't you ever spooked?"

"About what?"

"Working among loonies."

When Vanda doesn't answer, Samia guesses she's alone in feeling what she feels.

"Are you really not freaked out when a crazy woman smears her period blood all over the walls?"

"I don't know."

"Honestly, Vanda…"

Samia's cheeks are flushed with annoyance, her gestures suddenly brusque, full of anger and lack of understanding.

"… Maybe you're a nutter like them."

Vanda's laughter starts again and swells, until Samia looks at her and also starts laughing. She covers her mouth with her hand, self-conscious about showing her teeth when she smiles.

A nurse pops her head through the half-open door and wrinkles her nose.

"Are you going to clean Magalie's room or stand around laughing all day?"

Samia's laughter stops abruptly, while Vanda's face turns into a mask.

"You want to swap places with us?"

"You want to swap with me?"

The nurse disappears without waiting for an answer and, alerted by the shouts of another patient, rushes to the far end of the corridor. This ward is difficult. The weakest, most severely ill patients display their madness, like an open wound impossible to cauterize. Hence the closed doors and garden with wire fencing. Vanda copes with it better or worse depending on the day and leaves either in stitches or down in the dumps. Or sometimes indifferent, she switches off. She has tried and tested techniques for not thinking, not judging, not suffering – imaginary films with scripts she rewrites with minimal dialogue, and when the screams become too unbearable, she puts her earphones in and takes refuge in music. It's not allowed. The doctors have said it a thousand times: you have to be alert, ready to react. But, shit, sometimes it's just too much.

At the end of the day, Vanda goes down into the garden for a smoke. The weeds are taking over everything, even the wire mesh, which is a good sign.

Magalie is sitting on a plastic chair, drinking a can of Coke. There's some white froth at the corner of her mouth and her eyes look dense. Her toenails, peering through plastic flip-flops, are too long and twisted. Above that she's pretty, or has been. No older than Vanda, but damaged. As far as fashion goes, Vanda isn't much more elegant in her baby-blue uniform. She sits down next to her, lights a cigarette and stares at the horizon, speckled with bushes, which looks good at this time of evening. This wing faces west and is located high up on a hill. Lower down, you can see the rooftops of the other wings, century-old trees and, further away, the northern districts of the city. You can't really put loonies slap bang in the centre, can you? A few idealists did try, but nowadays, that is no longer the policy.

Vanda isn't afraid of Magalie. She's a little scared of Jean-Jacques, who always pops out of nowhere and gets his face too close to hers, with his stinking smile and slobbering laughs. But she quite likes Magalie. She doesn't know what happened to her or why she's here. Sometimes, when she talks to a medical member of staff, she looks perfectly normal and actually educated. But other times she goes off the rails. Sometimes she goes home for several months but when she comes back she looks even more wrecked than before, can't communicate, is hostile or delirious.

"You OK?"

"Shut up."

"I'm exhausted."

"Fuck off."

"Other than that I'm fine."

"Get lost."

Vanda's smile widens.

"I'm enjoying the chat, too."

"I said fuck off!"

Beyond the mound of brambles and rooftops, you can clearly see a patch of sea, royal blue. Vanda crushes her cigarette. When she stands up to leave, Magalie looks up at her and frowns.

"Are you off?"

"Yes."

"Bye, then, see you tomorrow."

"See you tomorrow."

Vanda turns her back on the fenced garden and disappears into the wing to change her clothes. If she doesn't get on with it, she'll be late – you'd think she's doing her best to screw up the reunion.

You Haven't Changed

Every time she catches the straw with her tongue, Simon thinks she's doing it on purpose and he's propelled back ten years.

"It's nice to see you."

That's not true. Nice isn't the right word at all.

Vanda usually wears bright red on her lips or else nothing at all. Today, it's nothing at all. Dishevelled and a bit on edge, she lifts her mane and secures it with a grip. Half her hair falls back down while the rest stays there, coiled between the plastic teeth. Later, she'll unclasp the grip, gather everything together and start all over again, of that he's certain. As for him, he's lost quite a lot of hair. You can't tell from the front but there's a bald patch, like a monk's tonsure, at the back. He's still managing to cover it up but gets totally depressed when he sees himself from the back in photos.

When they went out together, she wore jeans or fatigues, sometimes a daring leather or imitation leather skirt, like a disguise, hooded tops and black T-shirts. Often, a Breton shirt – she'd got a taste for stripes after seeing Charlotte Gainsbourg in *An Impudent Girl*. Today, she's wearing jeans, a black jumper and a scarf for oldies, grey, with checks. He studies it. He can't help it. It leaps out at him, probably because of his mother, the funeral, the assessment, the stocktaking and all that crap. The details come back to him and he lets them, feeling sorry for himself.

"I saw they closed La Machine à Coudre down."

"It may be just temporary."

"Still annoying. Where do you people go dancing?"

"There are other places. They haven't closed L'Arraché."

He whistles with surprise and laughs at the same time. She smiles to herself. L'Arraché is a real dump. Rotgut to wind up the evening. Talking about these places makes him emotional. He wonders if he'd like to take Chloé there.

Vanda bruised easily if someone knocked into her. He remembers her body all black and blue after a crazy pogo at La Machine.

He's glad she called him and wonders why she did.

He finds her coarse when she drinks her Coke through a straw. It annoys him that she slurps the bottom noisily, like a child. He can't remember if he used to like it – this quirk of hers, her way of not giving a damn about some things.

"You haven't changed."

"You have."

That makes him laugh and he hesitates to be offended.

"You think I look old?"

"Don't know. You look different. Serious, not much fun. What is it you do in Paris, again?"

"I'm a graphic designer."

"Do you enjoy it?"

He wonders if she actually gives a shit. Above all, he finds her question incredibly naive. Does he enjoy it? What planet is she on?

"Yes, I enjoy it. I make a nice living and my work is appreciated."

That sounds totally idiotic and he could swallow his own tongue – he just wants her to know he's made it, that he's happy without her, the absurd revenge of people who've been dumped. Even after seven years.

He remembers that he never dared introduce her to his mother. He was ashamed of being ashamed of her. But she was too unpredictable, she shone in only one circle and wasn't adaptable. They'd been turning around each other for a while when they finally grabbed each other at the Dock des Suds, one night when there was a concert – he hasn't listened to Patti Smith for years. Grabbed each other as if they were starving even though it was a time of plenty. Could have been the ecstasy that gave them that uncontrollable desire to touch each other, to follow the length of each other's body, feeling as though they were suddenly connected by invisible but palpable threads and veins. He hasn't touched that shit for ages. He took a little coke when he arrived in Paris, just for fun, to settle in, but then he stopped. He drinks a lot, on the other hand, often and too much. Chloé sometimes mentions it, but it's not like she doesn't drink like a fish herself.

The thing with Vanda lasted a while, then he went to Paris. No, that's not the right way of putting it. She dumped him, so he left – it didn't matter if it was to go to Paris or somewhere else.

Like Vanda, he went through art school: a dalliance, the thing to do for a talented young man who had some ability. In the end, he became a graphic designer and moved to Paris, where it all happens. The fan magazines he worked for here seem trivial now. In Paris, he became a pro, pretended he wasn't from the south and concealed what was left of his accent, of the sing-song. Now, Paris goes south, colonizes the wilderness and gets all excited on the terraces of trendy hotels. He finds that funny. But it doesn't make Vanda laugh at all.

"The rents have gone up because of these arseholes."

"Yeah, but they do some good stuff, too, there are some positive initiatives."

She looks at him as if he had shit all over his face.

"Yeah, you've definitely changed."

He's not so sure he's changed, perhaps he's just come out of himself. In any case, when he left this city, he was dreaming of clean lines, of clean pavements, and practically longed for the spick-and-span cities of the north. There are no straight lines here, either in the streets or in people's heads. Everything's up for debate and possible to alter, just look at the cycle lanes encroached on by flower-pots, bits of café outdoor seating and bins. Only the horizon over the sea is in a straight line, as well as the cuboid Mucem Museum. Even the buildings are lopsided – so much so that they keep tumbling down. Simon explains his viewpoint, about geographical evolution, demographic movement and the logic of the real-estate market. He doesn't necessarily agree with it, but that's reality so you have to adapt. He's not even sure he himself believes in the bullshit he's spewing or if he's doing it to wind her up, contradict her, to look clever. Getting a response is renewing a bond. He'd like to seduce her again, idiot.

She was so beautiful when they fucked anywhere they could find, from the toilets of L'Arraché to the Niolon coves.

At this time, the outside seating area is empty. The skinny waiter who looks like David Bowie picks up the ashtrays. Vanda fiddles with her glass and calls him to order a beer – two, Simon signals. Her arms rise up to the hair grip again and she unclasps it, freeing her mane. She shakes her head and her curls dance, slow and heavy around her face and on her shoulders. It's not a flirtatious gesture but rather a familiar movement that reassures her before she goes on to serious things. She thinks she no longer has the choice, that the clouds are going to burst and trigger the flood anyway.

"I imagine you want to see Noé."

"Noé?"

He squints and tries to place the name in his memory, but it's a blank. Like an imbecile, he pictures an ark and a bunch of animals, an association of ideas, but there's no echo, he doesn't understand.

"Who?"

"Your son. Isn't that why you're here?"

The End of the World

It's started again tonight. It's not always exactly the same dream but they're strangely similar. Not because of what they're about – their narrative threads are varied and numerous – but they're all based on the same thing: it's the end of the world. It's the end of the world and she's going to die, first her then Noé, or the other way round, sometimes both at the same time, and sometimes other people – faceless puppets – as well. Everyone's going to die. Tonight, it's extremely dangerous animals springing out and killing; bunches of snakes as large as tree trunks. And especially there's this dust with specks in it, deposits you mustn't breathe in but that are hard to avoid. Nobody mentions it on television and everybody acts as though nothing's happening and that makes it worse. In her dream, Vanda feels infinitely sad and dreadfully power-less. She tells herself that she'd never have thought this would happen to them, during this era, while she's still around and Noé is a child. She imagined that the end of the world would come in hundreds or thousands of years' time and that it wouldn't touch her. And yet here they are, it's happening now and is unavoidable. Once, they were being swallowed by a giant wave. They were on a deserted street, unpaved, like in a Western, and the wave was above them like an immense glass globe. As they were suddenly immersed, she saw Noé's eyes grow larger when he realized what was happening, and that tore her heart. With death imminent, the question was whether it was better for her to go before him so she could give him a few extra seconds of life, or after him so she could reassure him till the very end and spare him the sense of total abandonment in seeing his mother die. This morning, she thinks she can still get away from the deadly dust when a huge animal with no name nabs Noé in its teeth and flees. No matter how fast she runs, Vanda can't catch up with the monster: her legs are slow and limp, caught up in the slow-motion of the nightmare. The animal slowly turns and devours Noé before her very eyes. She screams and wakes up, panting with terror and above all with sadness. Tears unexpectedly pour out, she tries to catch her breath in the darkness, gets out of bed and rushes to Noé's bed. He's alive and stirs as she caresses him, and it's almost time to get up. She kisses him in the dark and wipes her face on his quilt so he doesn't feel her sadness, but she's inconsolable. There's a lump in her stomach, it's a dream but it's also more than that. It's a warning, a premonition – whatever shape the end may take, Vanda knows it's going to come.

She opens the curtains on the double doors and lets the grey morning light in. To ward off her anxiety, she switches on her computer and plays a track, something gentle they both like, but it doesn't take the sadness away, or the certainty of imminent death for her, her son and the whole of humanity.

Guest

The esplanade outside the train station is dotted with colours and lights. Chloé smiles but not for long, because a stinking guy walks right up to her and asks for a cigarette. He's got revolting dreadlocks, thick, sour-smelling sweat. The neckline on his vest hangs low over his chest and he wears several leather necklaces with medallions on his gleaming skin. His muscles are toned like those of a dancer and he's blocking her view with his frame. He can see very well that she's trying not to grimace, because she's not like that, she doesn't look down on him, she just wants nothing to do with him, for him to disappear, for him to take his cigarette, light it with her lighter, holding it in his revolting hands, then go away. Actually, he can keep her lighter, she's giving it to him. The guy sniggers, he's not stupid, he examines her from top to toe, deliberately, his eyes linger on her Repetto pumps then travel back up to her face. He hesitates to flirt with her, feels half-hearted about it, but it's force of habit, so breaking it would be too much of a shock, as if he'd got old or lost his knack, while she looks beyond him – he's not there any more, she doesn't want him to be there, and Simon's still not back, shit, how long does it take to buy cigarettes?

She can't understand how Simon can be originally from here. He's so elegant, so delicate. She's very close to his secret metamorphosis but doesn't know it. This isn't France, it's something else. She's not a racist, she doesn't want to say there are too many Arabs, but Arabs are all she sees everywhere. With woven red, black and white chequered plastic bags. Caps ridiculously positioned on the tops of their heads, acting as if they want to nick her phone and handbag – mocking, superior, humiliated. It's not just Arabs, it's everybody, actually. She feels hot and wonders if she hasn't brought too much stuff for just a few days. She feels nauseous again. She left the banlieue to go and live in Paris, not to come back to the same kind of place, where it's as though people get their clothes from rubbish bins or from wherever they can, or from the back of a truck. They're ugly. She'd deny this, of course, but that's exactly what she's thinking, deep down; never had she realized just how much she likes being surrounded by people who, if they're not naturally attractive, at least do what they have to do to be elegant, accessorized, and pay attention to how others see them. She's ashamed of feeling this way, she's left-wing.

"Sorry, there was a queue. Is everything OK?"

The guy walks away and goes to swipe a cigarette from someone else. Chloé lights hers with the lighter Simon hands her.

"It's an odd kind of arrival."

"Why? Did the guy bother you?"

"It's OK."

Simon turns towards the large church with the gilded

dome, which dominates the entire city, and presents it all to her with a somewhat theatrical gesture.

"See? It's beautiful, isn't it?"

There's certainly enough sun in your eyes. Glaring blue, beams that soften the rooftops and gild the flagstones. She relaxes and lifts her face to the light.

"Shitty weather in Paris."

Well, that's something, he thinks. Afterwards, he could take her to the *calanques*, even get his old scooter out. But after what? After the funeral? He's got to tell her about the kid, only he doesn't know how. He's been totally out of it since he heard, and can't even string two thoughts together. Particularly since he's had to handle the preparations for the ceremony, dig out memories, write something and call the funeral directors. A whole load of things he didn't know he could do, and which he's done like a zombie, obsessed with the news about this child.

Chloé takes him by the hand and puts his tormented expression down to the funeral.

"Are we going there straight away?"

"They're waiting for us outside the cemetery. My aunt's driving us. She's double-parked."

Chloé expected this, so is dressed in black. She never knew Simon's mother, or his aunt, or any of his family members, or even this city he's from. And yet they've been together three years.

The car smells of dog, and white hairs stick to their mourning outfits. His aunt is sorry, apologizes, talks a lot, and this allows Chloé to look at the city through the open window. She relaxes and squeezes Simon's hand.

*

He vaguely remembers the procession at his grandmother's funeral, but that was a long time ago, he was a child. Also his stepfather's, which was more recent. The avenues of Saint-Pierre are huge, the vaults towered over by obese umbrella pines and an abundance of creepers. The small mourning group has scared off the cats, which have sought refuge in the section where those who died for France are buried: rows of little white crosses with, nailed in the centre, photos of young men with a hint of moustache. The group turns off towards the east. The place is so big that he wonders if he should memorize the names of the dead along the way, so he can find his bearings the day he comes to place flowers on his mother's grave.

There are about twenty of them and Simon's almost surprised there are so many. He recognizes his family, of course, but sees friends of his mother he doesn't know. He skipped a large proportion of his mother's life. Many smile at him, she must have talked about him. He wonders what she said about her son, whether she complained about no longer seeing him very often or if she in fact realized that his adult life had made them drift apart.

He walks behind the car, holding Chloé's hand. His aunt is next to him and, behind her, his cousin, who took him in her arms when they met again. They're all wearing dark glasses and it's hard to say if it's because of the tears or the blinding sun that dominates the cemetery. Simon wishes he could live his tragedy in full, think of nothing except his mother and the sacred moments of his life with her. But all that comes to his mind is the photo in the living room, in which she's wearing the A-line dress. It's as if she's already frozen, and in a distant past on top of everything else. Maybe it's a way of fleeing from his last image of her as a corpse, he's not sure. Above all, he's thinking about the child and that takes up all the space in his head. He's alone with his secret, focused on the slowness of his steps so he can keep a metre behind the funeral car, with its open windows and the coffin adorned with flowers. His cousin's children are further back with their father, and the youngest – a girl – is picking the daisies growing between the pavement and the nearest graves. The eldest must be the same age as this son of his he hasn't met. Good God, this is turning his head inside out. He's swaying between utter joy and anger at not finding out sooner. He mentally talks to his mother, which is totally pointless since even long before she died he'd stopped telling her much – only trivial stuff, nothing personal, nothing important. Held together in his mourning suit, his skull feeling crushed by the pressure from all this self-consciousness, Simon's finding this tough. He scratches his eyebrows, a familiar gesture whenever he's anxious, and it gives him a hangdog look. Chloé clings to his arm.

He wonders how she's going to react when she finds out. He looks at her from the bottom up. She's perfect in her little black skirt and blouse with the Korean collar, holding his arm like a young wife, supportive in the face of life's trials. He wants to throw up. She's looking at everyone with an expression of mild surprise but trying not to make it too obvious. He understands perfectly well, even if he doesn't let on. She knows Simon didn't grow up on a council estate and didn't experience poverty, but today she senses the sadness of little lives, the contentedness of a successful family meal, of receiving a housing allowance. She calls it sadness to ward off contempt. He's not far from thinking the same thing, no wonder he left. He refuses to judge his mother, however, or his aunt and his cousins. He did it a lot before he left, confident he deserved more, although he was aware that his mother's encouragement, her hopes and her enthusiasm, made him that way – longing for more, imagining a different life, one that would make the eyes of those left behind sparkle. He'd like to have been self-made, but he owes his mother a lot.

He never once invited Vanda to his mother's. Of course, he's always liked to compartmentalize his life, it's a way of being in control of it, but that's not all. Vanda, the relationship that would mean his destruction, his social fall. No point of reference, a solitude ready for all kinds of eccentricity, a totally scary form of freedom. He didn't introduce his mother to Chloé either and he knows why it's not the same set-up. He did consider doing it a few times, when he went to meet her family in the suburbs. Not exactly upper crust, but with bookcases, a garden, parents dressed like him, highbrow newspapers lying around, a *Le Monde diplomatique* even in the toilet, as well as old Wolinski cartoons. Weekends in Normandy. The generation gap was practically non-existent. He felt grown up. He sometimes wonders if Chloé's family doesn't have a bearing on his love for her. She's his opportunity, his leg up. Chloé, on the other hand, doesn't want kids and has always been crystal clear about that. But he keeps kidding himself that someday she'll change her mind.

Simon doesn't like to mix his worlds and wonders why he agreed for Chloé to come. She'd never even met his mother, so why did he? At the same time, it makes him feel less alone. In any case, it's all chaos and he doesn't know what he wants, is suffering, wishing he could vanish or else curl up on a sofa. And all this light everywhere that gives the cemetery a touch of enchanted garden, it's almost indecent. He'd rather it rained on the stone virgins and cherubs, on his back and his head, and for the procession to break up as soon as possible.

The car comes to a halt and the men in black with high-gloss shoes take the coffin out.

His aunt gives a speech, tells stories about childhood, about a river and blossoming fig trees, about a full life and meeting Georges. Not meeting God – Simon told her not to. Shit, after all, his mother believed in nothing, so she doesn't have to put up with religious nonsense at her burial. The aunt's not convinced and joins hands in eloquent fervour. Then it's his turn and it's as if he's the one being thrown into the hole, he so wants to disappear. He smooths his bit of paper, his hands shaking like those of a first-time actor. He's decided on something quite short, a poem she liked and used to recite to him when he was a child. He realizes he still knows it by heart and that the words flow out by themselves, like a magic formula. He crumples the piece of paper and crushes it in the palm of his hand with his thumb, focuses his eyes on the wood of the coffin. He doesn't like the idea of decomposing and, as far as he's concerned, he'd rather be cremated. Nothing romantic, no ashes thrown into the sea or from the Golden Gate Bridge, please. Just being reduced to nothing, not to imagine himself as a corpse that's rotting away more and more as the months go by. Or, even worse, to be not completely dead and waking up under the ground, possibly with his cousin next to him, in a trauma worthy of Hitchcock's *Final Escape.* He lifts his head once he has finished, people are sniffing like mad, and he, too, is moved. He motions at the impassive strongmen, who slide his mother into the grave.

Simon clears his throat and explains he hasn't had the courage to organize something for people to get together afterwards. He's sorry but he'd rather gather his thoughts on his own and hopes everybody understands. He sees approving nods, sympathetic smiles and his cousin coming to hug him.

"We have to dash back to Nice, but it was nice to see you, despite the circumstances…"

"It was nice to see you, too."

"Are you going to stay?"

"No. Funny, your mother asked the same question."

His cousin gives his arm a squeeze and puts her head on his shoulder.

"Come and see us in Nice sometime, with your girlfriend."

Simon gives a little wave to his cousin's children even though he doesn't know them, and to her husband, whom he's met twice.

As they leave along the avenues of the cemetery, everyone comes to have a word with Simon, shake hands or kiss him. He barely listens but smiles politely, accepts the handshakes and sticks his face to flabby cheeks, revolted by all that cologne, that aged, made-up skin, those faces latticed with furrows. People gradually leave and Simon feels like he's fading a little more after each embrace.

As long as he hasn't told anyone about the child, he doesn't exist. He's not in the flesh. As long as he keeps his secret, there's nothing but his mother's death, relatives to kiss and a train ticket to return to Paris. Perhaps a drive to the *calanques*, so he can show Chloé.

Once everyone's gone, Simon, Chloé and the aunt head to the exit without talking. The aunt is sobbing and Simon wonders if it's because of her sister's death or her daughter's hasty departure.

He longs for a strong drink and a shower. He's sweating under his suit and the black coat it didn't occur to him to remove. It stinks of sweat and death but he holds on to his conceit. Simon's still hoping to look the part.

People's Smells

Vanda's found a window seat on the bus, Noé snug on her lap. Yesterday, her car broke down, but there's never anywhere to park at the flea market anyway. She wonders how she's going to get to work now. The bus is packed, people standing and practically falling over one another at every stop. She stares at a man's piercing blue eyes and long, fair lashes the colour of a Camargue horse. He's wearing a heavy scent, a musky cologne. She imagines he must have a date. Vanda needs smells, even bad ones. Smells speak to her, grab hold of her and root her in the world.

Sometimes, she can smell her own sex. It's often on the days when loneliness digs a hollow in her belly.

The smell of men. The smell of women.

The smell of the storm and suntan lotion. The smell of the city, on the days when bin collectors are on strike. Wild seagulls, giant rats rotting, their bellies up, unwashed men, beggars with pungent grime.

The smell of the sea.

And, above all, the smell of her son, of the sweat on his neck. His night breath, when he opens his mouth in his sleep.

Vanda realized very early on that she was alone, just as you're alone the day you die. She absorbed the grief of it until she turned it into an identity, a suit of armour. Other people matter a little, but they leave and disappear. Look at her best friend from primary school, the one with whom she used to play under the sheets, and the little gang at high school, whose chief concern was to get out of the place as soon as they could. She has no idea what happened to them. They didn't stand the test of time and absence. And the major love affairs, the kind that give your pulse a meaning, for the sake of which you think you can die, or that killed you when they departed. It's all bullshit: you don't die from it.

When her son was born and she held him against her for the first time, she felt something inside her snap. He was there and had no one but her. *He's going to love you all his life*, she kept telling herself, and she wasn't sure if it was something wonderful or a fucking curse.

Vanda doesn't understand the fragility of china, preambles and precautions. Consequently, for a brutal, solitary woman, a child – a child with eyes like a featherless bird, his translucent skin and his total dependency – wasn't something she was sure she could handle. The first thing she did was sniff him.

An old woman knocks against the man going on a date. She's wearing an anorak and a pair of leopard-print trousers. She smells of curry and candyfloss. Swearing at the motions of the bus, she shoves sweets into the mouth of a little girl – no doubt her granddaughter – glued to her legs. She holds one out to Noé and insists he take it in a language Vanda doesn't understand.

Smells speak to her at work, too. Gérard's freshly shaved cheeks, Fadiha's hair conditioner, the washing powder, the old fabric, the detergents. The heady breaths of antipsychotic drugs. Shit, fear, coffee. The perfumes of the women changing in the cloakroom, taking off their hospital uniforms.

But no one knows she always carries Noé's dirty T-shirt at the bottom of her handbag. It has his smell and she buries her face in it whenever the world gets too threatening. It's always been threatening, but Simon's arrival makes it even more so. She doesn't know exactly what he's bringing but she senses danger, a smell of cracked soil, of an oozing, craggy crater. Something's about to shift and she's not sure that her house-of-cards equilibrium can withstand the gusts.

At the flea market, she holds Noé's hand tight. The last thing she wants is to lose him in this sea of bodies, this open-air Fourth World where even the most insignificant T-shirt – even if it's dirty and torn – is sold on and laid out on the pavement. She sometimes thinks that this is where the revolution will start, but maybe poverty reaches a stage where it's too late for anger, so you kick into survival mode.

Noé stops in front of the stands with broken toys, sees a silicone dragon, marbles and a Lego boat with a firefighter in it.

"Come on, Limpet, it's not worth it, they're all broken."

"Please, Maman."

"I want to show you something better."

She's excited, imagines his joy and wants him to hurry. But Noé is six years old and the toys only cost a few centimes.

"Please, please, please."

Pouting like a sick kitten, he strokes the suspiciously green dragon. The woman selling the toys offers the lot for one euro. She also sells batteries and mobile phone chargers, and is already stuffing the toys into a plastic bag. Vanda gets annoyed and drags Noé away between the stalls. They zigzag to the entrance of the giant sheds where fruit and vegetables are sold. Noé deliberately scrapes his trainers against the ground, disappointed and sulking.

They walk past the assortment of yoghurts Vanda recognizes: the hospital desserts diverted by officials before they even reach the fridges. She knows the pattern of this kind of trafficking, officials who are so badly paid that they steal the patients' desserts so they can sell them here. She's already seen them at it, doesn't approve, but watches them without reporting anyone. She pulls Noé deeper into the belly of the market.

There are cries, singing and short, high-pitched sounds coming from the far end of a shed: the cacophony of a feathered menagerie. Noé's face opens like a window, his eyes wide.

Dozens of cages are stacked up, full of birds of every colour, from green parakeets to pheasant hens. A little further in, slightly concealed, there are scarlet macaws, linnets and long-tailed tits, lots of bird varieties it's illegal to sell.

Vanda waits for Noé's reaction and feeds on his joyful outbursts. She thought of Noé as soon as she discovered this unofficial market of birds. He dreams of going to the zoo, but she never has time and it's expensive. There isn't one nearby; it's almost an hour on the motorway. Besides, now her car's dead, it's just not going to happen.

The noise is deafening and the stridulations fill the entirety of this feathered black market. Sometimes, a seller covers a cage with a cloth so they shut up. There's a powerful smell of bird excrement that makes their noses sting. Noé is in awe, goes from cage to cage, calls his mother to show her a couple of sun-yellow lovebirds, then a blue tit. He laughs, tries to imitate the song of a parakeet and the clucking of a grey parrot. Then he freezes in front of a cage, his mouth half open. Vanda sees a delicate little bird with a red-and-black head and a glossy beige back.

"The young man has good taste. I'll do him a deal at one hundred euros."

The guy talking to Vanda looks like a musketeer. Moustache with curled-up edges, hair down to his nape, he's amused by the child's wonder.

"One hundred euros? For a bird?"

"It's a rare bird. And not the most expensive, madame."

Vanda's annoyed. She wanted to do something nice for Noé, perhaps even bring a bird home, but she didn't realize the creatures cost that much.

Her salary as a hospital cleaner isn't going to buy the kid an aviary of rare birds. But Noé's eyes are shining, he's talking to the bird in a whisper, won't let go of the wire netting and slides his fingers through it. So Vanda opens her handbag. Her heart is pounding. It's a lot of money. But when Noé puts his fingers through a tiny door and caresses the goldfinch's red head with the tips of his fingers, Vanda has no more hesitation.

I'm Going Back to Paris

"That's totally insane."

"I know."

Chloé bites her lip, paces up and down the living room, can't get over it, wishes this conversation had never happened.

"You didn't know?"

"No, I didn't."

"Shit! How could you not know?"

"We broke up, I left and never saw her again, end of story."

His forehead pressed against the window, Simon can't find anything else to add. He'd hoped Chloé would help him see things more clearly.

In silence, he goes to get two beers from the fridge but reconsiders and dives under the sink. He gropes around, positive he knows what he's doing, until his hand clasps a bottle of whisky. His stepfather had a taste for it and his mother didn't drink.

"There's nothing else I can say. I didn't know, that's all."

"But surely some of your mates stayed here, right? Didn't even one of them do the maths and wonder?"

"You know I cut all ties."

"Maybe he's not yours."

Simon finds the hopefulness of her question hurtful. He pours the whisky into two glasses and goes back to her. "Wouldn't you like that?"

"What do you mean?"

"I don't know. You look like you hope he's not mine."

"Obviously! Don't you?"

They stand, facing each other, their dissent back in the centre like a crappy tune the radio plays on a loop. Simon drains half his glass before saying, "You don't want kids, anyway, so you can't possibly understand."

"That's nothing to do with it."

They're grabbed by a clawing silence. Simon finishes his whisky in quick small sips, gagged by powerlessness, halfway between anger and collapse. Chloé studies sternly the outdated decor of the family apartment.

"Did you grow up here?"

"No. We moved when I was a teenager."

"Why have you never told me about your family?"

"I have told you about them, what did you want me to say?"

Chloé hesitates, puts her glass down on the coffee table and walks up to a wall of photographs. She can't bring herself to come out with what's eating her, but Simon understands perfectly well even if he pretends he doesn't. *You come from a family so different from you*, that's what he hears, and clearly senses that this upsets her view of him.

"How did you meet this woman?"

"We had mutual friends. Our paths also crossed at art school. But we didn't really get to know each other till later."

"Were you with her for a long time? Was she important to you?"

"Yes. And yes. I mean I think so. It was a long time ago."

Chloé shakes her head. She doesn't want to hear about this child. It's true that she doesn't want any as it is, Simon knows that. It's always hard to explain. No one wants to accept it. People just smile knowingly: you'll change your mind, you'll see, you're still young. It drives her crazy, all this idiocy, this tunnel vision, this single-mindedness, this impossible path people around her – not all, but many – refuse to take in order to understand. She doesn't want to have any. She has nothing against kids, nothing against those who want them, she just wants them to leave her alone. Only, at thirty-five, the pressure's growing, people keep dropping unsubtle hints, and it's the same questions on and on. Simon's like everybody else but there's something undecided, always, that shields them from actually doing anything about it. Simon would quite like to, he hopes, suggests, come on, why not, it would be great, but when it comes down to making a real decision, he stops there, or not there, as it happens, and that suits Chloé fine.

Once – actually no, many times – they had a row. She has a load of reasons, partly to do with money: they make a nice living, but in Paris that's not enough to have an extra room. She doesn't want them to be crowded, to sacrifice themselves and get lost. She's often heard this lesson about sacrifice, first and foremost from her parents. She likes her life, filled with adult activities and concerns appropriate for her age. No, she doesn't feel like getting down on all fours to play with little figurines, emit a constant stream of admiring exclamations, apparently doesn't feel like adopting the universal, mystical gestures of childbirth, of gleeful unconsciousness, or the doldrums of reproduction. They say she's selfish, but she rejects the accusation. It's no more selfish than wanting to reproduce and wallow in the qualities of a new being who owes us everything, the mirror image of our successes and a compensation for our failures. Deep down, what drives her crazy is having to justify herself. She doesn't want to and if she doesn't want to it'll be dire. But this now is another matter. This child does exist and he's not hers.

"What would you have done if you'd known back then?"

It's a good, complex question. Simon wonders if he wouldn't rather she got angry, because he's learned the tried and tested couple mechanism of dodging, running away, arguing back. But real questions that force him to think out loud are dangerous. He's projected into the past at full speed, history is reassembled through the prism of the future, which automatically makes it biased, but he tries anyway. Everything that came afterwards would have been different, he knows that and doesn't like the dizziness of might-have-beens. It's pointless.

Chloé continues to examine the apartment. They were so close and all it took was to return to his birthplace for a crack the size of a crater to appear, for her to look at him like a stranger, for him to consider her an enemy.

"I don't know what to say, Chloé. Only now I want to meet him."

"And after that?"

"What do you mean?"

"What will you want to do after you've met him?"

"I don't know. I haven't thought about it."

"You haven't thought about it?" Chloé gives a tired little laugh.

"Fucking hell, this just hit me at the same time as my mother dying, so I'm a bit lost here, can you understand that?"

Simon pours himself another glass and looks at her. Her short hair has regrown on the back of her neck. He wants to press his lips against it. He loves her neck, her socialite neck, and the shape of her shoulders under her sweater. He loves her lack of compromise, her way of living in the world, straight and wilful. He suddenly wants her to hold him in her arms, he painfully desires her. She walks up to the window and presses her forehead to the glass.

"I'm going back to Paris."

"You're leaving me all alone."

He regrets the weakness in his voice and the bitterness in this question that isn't a question.

"You're not a child any more. You actually have one of your own. So deal with it. I can't do it for you and I have to be back at work the day after tomorrow." To soften the blow, she goes to him and runs her fingers through his hair. "I'm not ready for all this. I'm leaving tomorrow and I'll wait for you at home."

Simon has a fleeting image of their apartment, not huge but well located, with its at the same time relaxed and sophisticated decor. He wishes he were there, back in the peace of it, the place he only left a few days earlier. He takes Chloé in his arms and pulls her to the sofa – it's a way of getting back in control. Or of not going to pieces, perhaps.

A few seconds later, they're naked and grabbing each other with a zeal that has no gentleness. But, despite Chloé's moves and her ready moistness, Simon can't get an erection and that brings out tears of anger. He thinks he's pathetic and even when Chloé comes under his fingers he doesn't feel any stronger. And yet her pleasure soared quickly, she tensed up hard, arched against him and didn't look away. Now, he won't let her touch him, pushes her hand away as she tries to give him a gentle handjob. Tired of his refusal, she falls asleep against him, a hand on his hip. He's constantly amazed at the way she falls asleep without warning.

Simon gets up, switches off the lights and goes back to sit next to her, the bottle in his hand. He watches her sleep, totally belonging to him and yet a stranger, far away. Her mouth half opens on the cushion, a sign that she's even faster asleep. He tucks a strand of hair behind her ear and strokes the back of her neck. Once again, he feels useless, feels sorry for himself as he whispers that he doesn't deserve her, even if she often makes him angry. Maybe she's right and they need to be back in the intimacy of their Paris apartment, to get away from this city that makes him so fragile, sucks him into its hot glue and messes totally with his head. He won't be able to sleep and the drinks he's knocking back won't help. It's going to be a long night and he's so alone.

Lucky Day

She said yes. Simon would have liked her to treat this as an occasion: for him it's a major moment. *Drop in late afternoon, after school,* she said, that's it. He didn't feel any particular excitement, any sense of sharing. His hands are shaking and he's sweating under his jacket. When he lifts the flaps to check, he sees halos of sweat staining his shirt, feels the dampness, closes his jacket again and blinks while turning his silver ring – thick and heavy – around his middle finger. He parked his scooter at the top of the steps. Amazing view, he has to admit. He notices the Château d'If on the horizon, and desolate islands behind it. He can't quite remember the name of every little island and he focuses on that as if it were of key importance in the moments that are about to follow. He doesn't understand how he could have forgotten them. He was so eager to leave that parts of his memory went kaput at his departure. The sea is calm, a grey-blue without depth, wrinkled.

When he took Chloé to the train station and kissed her at the edge of the platform, she smiled at him from afar. He was lost. He realized he hadn't even taken her to look at the sea. There wasn't enough time, or desire.

Because of the new checks, he wasn't able to go to her carriage, wheel her suitcase and wave to her once the train departed. Station goodbyes don't have the same feel any more, but it was actually a relief not to prolong the bitterness, the questions in Chloé's eyes to which he couldn't reply, his own culpability, that of being unable to explain, of never being in the right place at the right time.

He walks down the steps to the beach. The steps are wet, the binder between the stones is crumbling. They're as narrow as a wall-walk in a medieval castle. The sand is already creaking under his soles.

He guesses which hut is theirs: there are toys stacked up outside the closed shutters, little buckets and rakes, a broken robot, a rolled-up beach towel. His mother always yelled at him when he came back from the beach and got sand all over the apartment, but she would invariably shake, rinse and hang up – acts of habit, and reproaches like words of love.

The paint is chipped all along the doors, peelings of green are strewn on the concrete overhang, old planks are lying around, rotting. He pictures what you'd need to do to make the place liveable: he's thinking DIY and a pergola you can take apart, he who can barely put up an IKEA shelf. There's a hollow in his stomach, nausea, fear. He doesn't even know who the child looks like, he didn't dare ask Vanda to show him a picture, and yet she must have dozens on her mobile. He was too shaken, incapable of knowing how he was supposed to act. He said yes. Yes, I want to meet him. Even his name, he didn't repeat it aloud, the name chosen by someone else, not him. He now repeats it softly, *Noé, Noé*, it's a nice name. He catches himself being joyous in the midst of the oppressive anxiety. The names of the islands aren't coming back, he stumbles over the void, the gap in his memory, it annoys him terribly but he refuses to get his mobile to find the answer. The answer belongs to him, he searches in the void of his memory, with rage, knowing that finding the names will provide relief, a kind of mental peace – a victory.

He hears them before he sees them, a harmony of voices above the railing, and the shapes that appear in the recess of the stairs, the child ahead, followed by his mother, who's carrying his school bag. Simon watches them come down, well, above all he quickly studies the kid, he's beautiful, this little boy: his hair, too long, makes him look like an escapee from the seventies, a brown lock almost hides one of his eyes, a Magikarp sweatshirt and hands waving about to make his point, he's still very little. Simon's shaken to the point of terror. He suddenly wants to vanish in their eyes, be able to observe the child in secret, familiarize himself with his gestures before meeting him.

Vanda notices him first. A hand gesture, an expression of surprise, you'd think she'd forgotten he was coming. She's carrying an electric-blue bag with large handles that seem to be sawing into her shoulder; he wonders what's inside it. The two of them walk towards Simon and the child keeps telling his story, it's about a playground game, something his teacher said to him, Simon doesn't understand exactly what it's all about, but he listens to the child's voice, his excitement, as he describes the teacher's reaction. If Noé has seen Simon, he's not paying particular attention to him. There are often people still strolling on the beach when he gets back from school, people he knows and strangers. He breaks off his story when Vanda kisses Simon on the cheek before unlocking the green door and opening the shutters in full, wedging them against the wall with stones on both sides. Noé asks no questions but looks at the man, alerted by his insistent gaze.

Vanda goes into the hut as if this didn't concern her, goes to put her bag on the bed.

"Hi, Noé," Simon says.

His voice has strayed off course, not as deep as he'd have wished. He thinks of Darth Vader, feels like an idiot, looks deep into the eyes of the boy, who hasn't moved.

"Hi."

"I'm Simon."

The kid doesn't reply but looks at him without animosity, with what he imagines must be curiosity. Simon doesn't know whether to extend a hand or else crouch and hug him – he'd like to, but children hate that, at least that's what he remembers. Unfamiliar adults who slobber over your face, overpowering perfumes, clammy skins, he remembers. Skin is something intimate, even on the face, so he stands motionless, with a smile he's trying to imbue with all he's thinking, his joy and quite a lot of other emotions like that.

Vanda comes back out with two beers wedged between her index and middle fingers and a glass of grenadine in the other hand. It's a mustard glass, with a logo Simon doesn't know. She sits at a distance, on the boundary where the pebble beach becomes sandy.

"Get a towel, Limpet, our bottoms won't get so sore."

Simon goes to Vanda, takes a beer without saying a word. The backwash is very gentle, marks a rhythm to which he clings, to quiet down the irregular beats throbbing all over his body. He sweats even more but breathes more easily. When the child comes back, the three of them sit on the stones, facing the sea. An old, fat, dark-haired woman goes into the water, her skirt lifted, and walks along the shore, far from them. It makes Simon smile: his grandmother used to do the same.

"It's good for varicose veins," he says and immediately regrets it.

The boy sits down next to his mother, who's in the middle, and who hands him his glass of grenadine. He's very careful and doesn't spill anything, drinks in small sips. Every now and then, he leans forward and steals a glance at Simon. He very quickly returns to his mother, his eyes brooding over her as if she were about to disappear. He grabs her wrist and, with his other hand, travels up her tattoos, which makes his mother giggle. A knowing, complicit giggle. Simon watches what looks like a ritual. Eyes shut, the kid draws the patterns with the tip of his index finger and guesses them by name.

"The red rose, the crocodile, the wavy bracelet."

"Not so quickly."

He goes back down, feels her elbow, strokes the crook of her arm. "The crocodile's mouth is here."

Vanda has trouble keeping a straight face, the child's finger is tickling her.

Simon feels uncomfortable. He's bothered by this game, too physical, almost amorous. He's got no place here. He wishes Vanda would say something: he was hoping for a conversation, confessions. He imagined words, hesitations, maybe tears, why not? He redirects his eyes to the horizon and to the woman walking in the water. Vanda and her son's whispering giggles are making him angry. He downs his beer in a single gulp.

"The clover!"

Simon stares at the islands, digs his memory to bring out the names, but the more he searches, the deeper he sinks. The clover… *Lucky day*, she said when he'd asked. They were naked, wrapped around each other after love-making, in her room, on the fifth floor in Rue de Tilsit, no terrace but rooftops you could get to through the window, dangerous but intoxicating. She'd throw her cigarette butts down from up there, heedless of passers-by. What lucky day? She didn't answer questions, especially if asked too directly. She'd feint, spin around theories, toy with alternatives. And to think that he happily put up with these mysteries, as long as he solved others. Her pleasure spots, her intimate geography, the softness, the hardness, the moistness, the quivering. Remembering it makes him nauseous, embarrassed – he's grown so old, he doesn't recognize this stranger, an amateur in love. There's something about desire that seems shameful to him when it's not controlled. It seldom is, in actual fact, and he's always found this folly of excess disturbing. It was she who was all rage and outbursts. He brushes imaginary dust from his jacket, which, where he comes from, makes him look stylish. But his jacket is out of place on this beach, impractical, and he's worried it'll get sea-sprayed. He feels confused – the irritation, the situation he's definitely not in control of. He should relax, he listens to this alien intimacy in the hope of understanding it, but what he sees above all is that he's not part of it, that he has no place in it.

"The irises…"

The kid's hand on his mother's shoulder, its delicate slope towards her neck, to the stems and petals dressed in skin. Simon's choking. He leans towards the child, wants to burst the bubble.

"Has your mother told you?"

His tone is really abrupt and hoarse, almost angry. The boy's face expresses nothing, as if Simon counted for nothing. But he opens his eyes. "Yes, I know. You're my father."

His little hand continues on its incursion, stops on the nape of Vanda's neck, under her curly mane. "The dice, six and four."

He closes his eyes again. Vanda lets out small laughs, sonorous, whistling approval. Simon unbends and stands up, so she turns a surprised face towards him. "Are you leaving?"

"No, I'm not leaving. I'd like another beer."

"Go on, you can go in, they're in the fridge. Get two."

His entire body relaxes as he walks away from the mother and child. He shakes himself, has recovered the fluidity of his movements by the time he reaches the hut, after getting stiff sitting down cross-legged on the pebbles.

The first thing that strikes him is the darkness and, straight afterwards, the smell. No windows – he gropes around to illuminate the cave. The switch is connected to several little lamps and to a string of coloured bulbs. They're not very bright, but the light is soft; he makes out a large bed, a small one against the other wall, but covered with so much stuff that the child can't be using it very often, a shower cubicle with a water hose and no head. Immediately to the left, a sink, a camping stove and a small fridge wallpapered with stickers. A toilet, no doubt, behind a plastic curtain. Everywhere, a mess, the coffee table cluttered with dirty plates, a full ashtray, crumpled clothes, heaps emerging from blue bags at the foot of the beds, threatening to collapse – she must do their laundry at work. One room. And a cage standing on the floor, near the head of the small bed, with a bird inside, singing. There's a smell of cumin, of damp, of chemical toilets. Simon stands there, stupefied, in the pale beams of yellow, red, green and blue lights that suggest a patron saint's day. He takes two beers from the fridge, looks for a bottle opener in a jar that contains all the cutlery, rummages around, unearths it from under a wet cloth.

When he re-emerges, the sky is pink and cloudy, like a cake shop. Orange and violet streaks accompany the sunset. There are just the three of them left on the beach: the old woman's disappeared. Crouching on the edge of the water, Noé is collecting small things in the palm of his hand. Simon makes out, against the light, like a shadow puppet, his lock of hair falling and sticking out. He sits next to Vanda.

"Why don't you get an apartment?"

Vanda extends her arm to catch the beer without looking at him. "We're fine here."

"It's a bit small, though, isn't it?"

He's instinctively cautious. The belly of the hut spoke of Vanda, way beyond its dilapidated state.

"I can't afford to get anywhere larger."

"Come on, with a housing allowance you can find a decent place, not huge but with a bathroom, a room for him."

He senses her stiffening, every bit of her hardens. "Who asked you? You come here to criticize?"

"No, of course not."

"I shouldn't have let you in."

"Wait, Vanda, I didn't mean to upset you, I'm sorry."

"*A decent place...* You're pathetic."

Contempt crimps her lips, like a snarl, ready to bite. She fixes her eyes on the pebbles. He clears his throat.

"You understand, he's my son."

Vanda's contempt turns into hilarity. A frenzy of laughter shakes her. She's scary when she laughs so loud, even Noé is looking up.

"OK, get out."

"Shit, Vanda..."

"You've seen him, you're happy. Now go back to Paris."

She's still laughing, but her tone is categorical.

Noé approaches, his palm filled with translucent green pebbles, bits of glass polished by the sea. He picks one and gives it to Simon.

"It's almost too dark to be able to see, I can't tell it apart from the grey ones."

"It's beautiful, thank you."

In the palm of his hand, the small shard of rounded glass burns his skin. He slips it into the pocket of his jacket, promises himself never to lose it. Night is almost here. So are the mosquitoes, because of the dry seaweed, the stagnant rock pools. Because of climate change, heatwaves in the middle of February, because of the ongoing climate change.

Simon gets up, a knot in his stomach. He watches Vanda pick up the bottles and the empty glass of grenadine.

"I want to ask you something."

"Go ahead."

"It's crazy, I've forgotten the names of the islands."

But she doesn't have time to reply before Noé jumps in. "Pomègues on the left, Ratonneau on the right, and the little island of Tiboulen at the end."

The knot in his stomach loosens, it's obvious, how could he have forgotten? His entire childhood rises in his belly, hearing these names from the mouth of the boy moves him even more than he'd like it to. He lets it wash over him, his helmet at his elbow.

"Bye, Noé."

"Are you coming back?"

Vanda replies in Simon's place. "No, he has to go home."

The boy waves at him then goes to the hut. He's already forgotten him. But Simon hears the names of the islands echoing in his voice. Vanda follows her son, turns to say goodbye before going through the door, the bottles threaded on her fingertips, monstrous appendages, overly large paws.

Simon drags his feet to the top of the steps, there's sand in his shoes.

He starts his scooter, slowly drives back up the street.

Despite the haze and sense of unreality, Simon knows perfectly well that he's in the process of getting himself into a fucking mess.

Bursts of Anger

There's tension in the air, smocks pass each other and hurl invective, patients are in a foul mood and there's a crisis on every floor. Some know, others don't. You can hear Jules's cries as he tears the sheets from his bed and wraps himself in them, the hollow laugh of Nina, the oldest of the patients, who hasn't been out for ages, doesn't even hope any more to live anywhere but here, her home. Yesterday morning, a patient died in the shower. No one saw him slip and faint, his head in the plugged shower tray filled with warm water. A few centimetres of stagnant water were enough for him to drown. As usual, there weren't enough carers, and today the hospital comes under administrative supervision, so there are consequences: there are going to be further cuts in staff numbers, the first names have already been dropped. The connection between the patient's death and the cut in staff numbers makes anger unavoidable. That's pushing cynicism too far, so there's a strike brewing. Vanda doesn't know if she'll take part even though it's risky – she's not on the list yet but she could be. The HR manager has warned them that those on provisional contracts can't afford to strike, that *there will be sanctions,*

I can assure you. A lot of people hate the bitch and her arrogance.

In the lobby of the wing, trade unionists have gathered, arguing with officials, getting heated. Even the timidest ones admit that they can't carry on like this. Around them, the patients are expressing either outrage or surprise: some are in a position to understand and add their anger to that of the carers; others, too ill, sense the agitation and are worried by it, keep spinning around, smoking one cigarette after another, asking questions on a loop, but don't listen to the answers. It's been going on for too long, escalating, it's as if the decision-makers are playing with fire, enjoying pushing the boundaries. It's anyone's guess if it's the patients who are going to die first or the exhausted carers, a large arena where each is fighting, not knowing if it'll be better for them to go it alone by looking for an escape route or join the others in taking a stand. Here, in Vanda's wing, it's a patient who died. But in Wing 17, a nurse killed herself last year. *You're lucky,* the HR manager says, *most of you are still employees.* Bullshit, almost an insult. She throws on the conference table a newspaper to which no one pays attention at first. Vanda approaches and looks through the articles on the open page until she finds the link: two employees of a large retailer refused to work on Sundays and have just been fired for serious misconduct.

Several nurses have been spending their Saturdays demonstrating month after month as it is. You know them by the fluorescent yellow security vests lying on the gloveboxes of their cars, by their faces that grow harder by the day, by certain grazes, and by their hatred of police and the government, seldom equalled in this job where some officials have claimed for ages to be apolitical as an excuse for their inaction. Today, everyone's anger converges, mixing those who've been shouting in the desert for years and those who've just found out. They're inches away from an explosion and the HR woman's not stupid, Vanda can hear it from her suddenly high-pitched voice, her arguments, which no longer hold up. Look, she's now scratching the crook of her arm – a stress-related attack of eczema. It makes Vanda smile, a small bit of revenge. With her tortoise-like head and her blazing youth, she triggers murderous thoughts in all the staff.

Vanda turns away from the crowd, goes out to smoke a cigarette in the garden. Magalie's still there, she's been rooted to the plastic chair for several weeks, she's just moved it under the garden's only umbrella pine. In psychiatry, the immovable borders on fixation. Vanda draws near but not too near, catches the shade of the skinny branches, lights her cigarette and spits the smoke out in a deep sigh. The silence in the garden is doing her good after all the shouting indoors, and she's grateful to Magalie for her ability to keep quiet. The turmoil postpones the time when you have to clean the rooms with bleach and telescopic brooms. Anger brings professions together, even the doctor's come out of his office to support the team – he experiences the patient's death as a personal failure. There's less of a chance that he could get fired, of course, but the officials note his presence anyway. He once spoke to Vanda in the corridor. She'd just comforted an anxious patient, had got the guy in pyjamas to drop his anger with a few words and the promise of a coffee. The doctor slowed down, studied her like a living creature – and not like a part of the furnishings.

"Are you a cleaner?"

It was a stupid question, what with her smock and her trolley it was blinking obvious, she didn't reply.

"I only ask because… Have you considered training as a nursing assistant? You're good with patients."

She wished she didn't give a damn, but it was nice to hear. Besides that, it was complicated to try and explain to him that applying for training, at the moment, would make all the staff at the Pôle temping agency laugh themselves stupid. Macron says you just need to walk across the street to get a job – well, whatever – no way is she letting go of her hospital work to train in anything at all. "You're entitled to training leave, you know? This is the public sector."

It was as if he'd read her thoughts; not so out of touch with reality, the doctor.

"I'm not permanent staff."

He sighed, shook his head: obviously he wasn't in support of the public policies regarding shitty contracts.

For a long time, Vanda didn't envy permanent staff, stuck in a job, a place, at the mercy of orders and changes, sort of part of the walls. Despite the insecurity of her position, she liked the freedom it allowed – the vestiges of a chaotic adolescence when commitment meant mental prison. It's different since she's had Noé. It's not that she wants a job for life at all costs, but her circumstances involve a whole load of worries she was shielded from before. Last time, the woman at the Pôle agency looked at her tattoos with an annoyed expression. She wasn't being nasty, after all she didn't give a damn, but she did tell her that it wasn't ideal for getting a job.

"Is it really a problem for doing the cleaning?" Vanda asked sarcastically.

"Since there are many of you, they prefer those who are best presented. It's all right in hospitals but there are hotels that don't allow it."

She told herself she didn't give a shit about hotels, she was fine at the hospital, but she felt a deep-seated rage burn in her throat, a feeling of unnatural selection in charge of employment. The world of work traded in dreams, she'd known that for a long time. Crazy how women who worked in the arts could parade a body tattooed up to their ears, people found that trendy and artistic, but for a job as a cleaner they thought she was just out of jail or that she couldn't behave properly. And yet her tattoos are delicate, luminous, there are many flowers, and they cost her a great deal, actually, a stack of overtime. Especially the fairy on her shoulder.

The doctor didn't insist, simply smiled, halfway between friendliness and evasive embarrassment, a slightly dizzying familiarity: the guy saw the picture, so did she, in the same boat but not the same position, admiral or stoker, in the end it's not the same. But perhaps they could fight the ship owner together. She went back to work first, freeing him from feeling obliged to add some condescending crap. Ever since, he always says hello when he sees her.

In the shade of the large pine tree, she smokes in silence, a knot in her belly. The school timetable means there are plenty of places where she can't work. Here, she can juggle her shifts, it's not slavery yet – a luxury. Thierry comes up to her.

"Are you OK?"

"My car still won't start. I don't know how I'm going to get it fixed."

"Shit, I'm sorry. Maybe ask Jean-Marc. He's good at mechanics."

"Not bad."

In actual fact, she's almost certain she'll never dare ask Jean-Marc anything, and for lots of reasons. She hates asking for help and she'd have to show him her home – the car broke down by the handrail above the beach – besides, Jean-Marc is rather clingy. Not mean or anything, but she wouldn't want to be indebted to him in any way.

"Are you striking, Vanda? We're counting on you."

She doesn't know what to reply, thinks about Noé, about their hideaway, and also about Simon, in a generic way, like an additional threat. Magalie sniggers.

"Your strike isn't going to change anything. Nobody gives a shit."

Thierry approaches, pretends he hasn't heard, so she insists:

"We can drop dead. And you can drop dead, too. You're worth almost as little as we are."

"Magalie—" Thierry starts.

"Shut up. You can also drop dead. Come on, give me a light."

He approaches and sticks his lighter under Magalie's cigarette. At the same time, he takes a packet from his nurse's uniform and lights one for himself. The worst of it is that she's right.

"That's not a reason for doing nothing."

"Oh, really? Then go ahead, go get your eyes gouged at the demonstration, see if that helps you at work afterwards."

"I know it's hard for you at the moment, what with the trial starting—"

"Oh, shut the fuck up. Actually, I'm not even talking to you. Drop dead."

Vanda can't help smiling and Thierry follows suit, laughter appears in their fed-up expressions, and even Magalie joins in, except that her laugh sounds like the creaking of a very old car door, and her teeth are really rotten. Vanda wonders what this trial thing's about. Cleaners don't read the patients' files, even if they sometimes know more about them than some nurses. She wants to ask but her curiosity is interrupted by the ringtone of her mobile. Vanda picks up and takes a few steps away from the others, as far as the fence. She stiffens. By the time she comes back under the tree, her face is closed.

"It was the school, my kid's sick."

"Then go," Thierry says.

"The head of department's going to rant, fuck, this really isn't the best time."

"Have you got an alternative?"

"No."

"Then off you go, I'll take care of it. You know she's not going to give me a hard time. It's twenty years I've been working with her."

Magalie keeps laughing on her own, back in her own world. Vanda's hesitation only lasts a few seconds. She smiles at her colleague and dashes to the tea room door, then turns back.

"Hey, Thierry, I'm in."

"What?"

"The strike, I'll be with you guys."

There's a smell of decomposing flesh on the 97 bus. It's running at full speed on the stretch of motorway between the districts in the north and the city centre: there are no traffic jams at this time. And there's a clear view of Notre-Dame-de-la-Garde, which stands increasingly taller as you approach. Not many people on the bus, but there's a young man listening to rap on his smartphone, the sound turned up to the maximum. Vanda listens and grimaces – lyrics about gangsters and police, whom the singer fucks like a bitch, everything through a vocoder, the tool for guys who can't sing. It's pissing her off. The others are looking at one another, everybody's hacked off, but no one dares say anything, everybody then studies their feet or a dot on the horizon. After a while, Vanda ends up going up to him.

"Don't you want to put on your headphones?"

"What?"

The guy leans over her, his expression very threatening, his body language ostentatious.

"What are you saying, sister?"

Ah, it had been a while. Her skin, her curly hair.

"I'm saying, your music is pissing everybody off. And I'm not your sister."

"I can do whatever I like. Go home and clean that stuff off." He points at the tattooed iris peering out of her sleeve. "You're an embarrassment to your race."

Vanda gets angry but then suddenly feels deflated, not from fear but tiredness.

"Shut the fuck up."

She turns her back on him and goes to find a seat as far away as possible. The guy's eyes are popping out of their sockets.

"What was that you said, you fat bitch?"

"I'm not talking to you. Drop dead!"

Borrowing Magalie's response makes her laugh, a laugh that's loud and mad enough to scare the idiot with his shitty music and his king-of-the-world pretentiousness, even though he's as screwed as she is. He gives her both hateful and timid looks, insults her but from a distance. An old woman in a veil gives Vanda a brilliant, complicit smile. When the bus brakes at the entrance to the city centre, a small black lump rolls down the vehicle: a dead rat, for real, and no one pays any attention – the miracle of habit. The guy gets off before Vanda and when she leaves he's already vanished. She dives into the metro. Afterwards, she has to catch another bus. When she finally reaches the gate, she checks the time: almost two hours door to door, from the hospital to the school. She grits her teeth, thinking about the smell of burning in her car, the impression that the wreck has uttered its final word and that from now on it's going to take an extra hour to get to work in the morning, and there's no possibility of mechanical repairs.

When she fetches Noé, he's as hot as a brioche, his eyes half shut and his cheeks red. So limp that she has to carry him halfway and hold him up on the stone steps.

She gets some Doliprane in a sweet pink paste into him, undresses him, and he falls asleep even before he's completely flat on the bed, his face buried in his prehistoric cuddly toy. Vanda brings the door shutters together, in a summer half-light. She rolls herself a joint with a small stub Jimmy left her the other night, takes a few puffs and places it delicately in the ashtray. Even though she's not ill, she allows herself to go to bed as well – afternoon sleep is rare and precious, it reminds her of Tangier, the white heat that makes you dizzy, the feverish inebriation triggered by light when it becomes solid. Through the gap between the shutters, she loses herself in the blue, then closes her eyes, her hands crossed between her thighs, body huddled up. Her hair spreads on her pillow in a star pattern, she looks like an Orthodox icon.

Sister. It's not the first time people have thought she's an Arab. Sometimes an Italian. It's true that she's dark-skinned, and then her eyes, something in her general appearance. Maybe she is half Arab, it's possible, but she has no idea, her mother was always quiet on the subject and since Vanda hasn't spoken to her for fifteen years, she's certainly not going to find out now. In any case, she doesn't give a shit.

That man's return, on the other hand, is a hell of a thorn she's going to have to tear out, a thorn at least the size of a triceratops's horn. She wishes she could sleep, too, like Noé, let herself go, yield to fever, let other people make the decisions, organize, count, anticipate, bite. She'll call the doctor later, or perhaps not at all; maybe he'll feel better tomorrow, kids bounce back quickly. Vanda adapts her own breathing to that of the sleeping child, finds a rhythm, her eyes shut. She calms down but remains awake, on alert, ready to pounce.

A Woman Like You

Last summer, the owner of their hut let their hideaway. In the summer, you can let this kind of shelter for a fortune, even though it's by the cliffs and has no windows, to rich people who want a garage for their Zodiac or a place to crash on their way back from fishing. Old people here generally don't like renting to strangers who are just passing through, but you have to make a living, right? Vanda and Noé had to leave, pack their stuff and put it at the far end of the hut before going to see if they were welcome somewhere else. Thanks to a colleague at the hospital, Vanda found a gig on a campsite, in Porto-Vecchio. Perfect for Noé, she told herself. In exchange for her work she was entitled to a few hundred euros, return tickets and a bungalow under the pine trees for two months – the kid could use the pool and even join in with the activities. There were pizza nights, pétanque, karaoke, pedalos on the artificial lake. It wasn't a large campsite, gravelled paths and families, umbrella pines, a few cork oaks with swollen barks and names carved on the trunks despite the sign at the entrance. Concrete toilets surrounded by flower boxes. Lavender that attracted wasps and bees, a convenience shop with overpriced items – washing power, toothpaste, biscuits, local cured meats, ice lollies and soft drinks. A cash-in-hand job, of course – Vanda knows the drill.

It wasn't exactly by the sea but not far from it, you had to walk twenty minutes or so through dense, rasping undergrowth, chalky stones between knobbly bushes. Vanda had never set foot in Corsica. She found it beautiful, luminous, hostile.

It wasn't easy in the beginning: she had to give directions, man reception, flag up problems and clean the toilets. She wasn't alone and her tasks varied according to need. The work wasn't a problem, but minding a five-year-old kid at the same time was a challenge. When it was quiet in reception, he could play next to her, but the rest was a true juggling act. Sometimes, she'd leave him with a family of holidaymakers, and that was at the same time a relief and a wrench, the fear that something bad might happen to him, the feeling of having abandoned him. Noé would return from the beach more tanned, happy, the folds of his skin full of sand that flowed down the shower tray. She'd say thank you, accept without flinching the embarrassed or judgemental smiles of the parents. When they left, they'd all wonder about the future of a child carted around like that, with a mother who was too busy to spend an hour on the beach with him. Not mean questions and not as harsh a judgement as she imagined, above all they felt sorry for her, they weren't rolling in it either. And yet she wanted to stuff their mouths with sand, that pale, golden sand that stuck to her son's skin, stuff it down their mouths till they choked.

Luckily, she had one day off a week. Only, the exhaustion after working for six days made her sleep until late morning. If Noé woke her up, full of expectations, he'd receive the rage of insufficient sleep, the anger of powerlessness, like when he spilled the coffee. She shouted, sometimes cried and fell asleep again, leaving Noé to rummage through the cupboards, eat crisps and play with her phone. She'd surface after midday, complaining about the heat, make two sandwiches and let him drag her to the pool. In the evening, she'd put on a dress with straps and ask for a lift to the harbour, her son in tow – it wasn't bad. They'd play at being tourists, she'd buy him an ice cream. She'd stop outside restaurants, read the menu and pretend to hesitate. Sometimes, she'd nick things from the plates of the diners after they left, before the waiters cleared the tables. A handful of fries, a cake. It made Noé laugh but he was also scared. Sitting on the wall in the harbour, they'd munch their booty. On the night of 15 August, Noé discovered the beauty of fireworks. She enjoyed his childish joy, was sorry she hadn't taken him to see them sooner.

In the harbour of Porto-Vecchio, the sound system blared songs by I Muvrini. Sexy young women strolled around, ponytail on the side, in Converse trainers of every colour. Groups of young men sniggered, couples formed. Families arrived, got the kids down from their shoulders, shouted contradictory instructions – *have fun, stay here, come back, get off me.* Vanda watched the agitation, the others, the way you peep through a keyhole. A stranger, a voyeur.

And then came the night of the dance.

She danced with Noé – they were beautiful, she in her paper-thin dress and he, tanned, hair bleached from the days in the sunshine. They laughed because of the music, the people, the dizziness from all the spinning. Vanda, because of the drink. Unable to drink mojitos at an outside table like the young women giggling in a gang, Vanda took out her little plastic bottle filled with vodka. A new track started, an old song, Jean-Jacques Goldman, everyone knew the lyrics. That's when she saw the owner of the campsite leaning against the bar. Jeans and his best shirt, pelvis sticking out. He was checking her out with a crooked smile, eyes shining, and she could immediately tell he fancied her. She didn't really like that, even though he was a good-looking guy. The thing is, when a man fancies a woman, it creates an obligation. It's stupid and, over time, things change, but sometimes a woman who doesn't know the rules of the game gets branded, especially when her circumstances depend on the man's goodwill. He gestured at her, turned to the girl behind the bar and ordered two beers. Vanda decided she didn't have much of a choice, but it could turn out to be nice, he didn't look like an arsehole, was always polite when he saw her at the campsite, polite and respectful. He turned to the girl again and ordered a grenadine for Noé. That reassured Vanda. The owner held the grenadine out to the boy, grabbed the two beers and came to sit on the wall nearby. Vanda followed, took her beer and clinked, Noé was happy, he was blowing bubbles through his straw and the music was so loud no one could hear him and tell him off. The boss asked Vanda how work was going, if she liked Corsica, if it was her first time here, that kind of thing. He wasn't really listening to the answers but looking at her intensely, she knew that look – she had to play it carefully, she didn't want to go to bed with him but didn't want to make an enemy of him either. Afterwards, he talked a lot about himself, about the pressure of running a campsite, and went around the houses to find out why she was here alone with her son. Check out if there was a guy in the background, one who was waiting somewhere, and if he could try his luck. It wasn't exactly subtle but not entirely repellent either, only banal and annoying, she was getting tired of the smile, pretending doesn't last long with Vanda. On top of that, he stood very close to her while talking and twice brushed her thigh with the back of his hand. It just went with what he was saying, a tactile kind of guy. To cool him down, she talked about his wife, who ran the shop, but that didn't discourage him. She wasn't quite sure what she wanted.

She said she was working tomorrow and Noé was sleepy, so he offered to drive them back. It was late and she was exhausted, she said *yes, OK, thanks.* When she gathered her hair to move it to one side the guy shook his head with admiration, with a totally obvious expression, as if she'd lifted her dress to show him her arse. Noé fell asleep in the car. The man stopped talking, but his silence was noisy. The night was too hot, with not a breath of air despite the proximity to the sea. The guy's silence was teeming with desire, she pulled her dress as far down over her knees as she could, wondering if she fancied fucking him. Maybe yes: he had large, firm hands, a face with high cheekbones, a strong but not protruding jaw.

A good-looking man, not very young, but hungry rather than worn out. It was hard to tell, his desire was too pushy for Vanda's to surface. So her first thought was to shield herself from it.

He slowed down at the entrance to the campsite and drove slowly to Vanda and Noé's bungalow. She leaped out of the car before he could turn off the engine, but he calmly got out and carried Noé, who was still asleep. With his broad shoulders, he lifted him as if he didn't weigh anything, picked him off the seat gently. His smile told Vanda to lead the way – and, especially, the way into the bungalow.

Once Noé was put on his bed, the small space of this miniature house became all too evident, their breaths blended together even though they weren't close to each other. Vanda now wanted him to leave. She felt that discomfort in her belly, when you're aware of a situation you didn't want to arise, but blame yourself for getting into. She came out of the small bedroom and he followed her. No word had been uttered since the drive. She tried to remember the last words they'd exchanged, as if she could take up the conversation where it had been left off, break the unease and escort him to the door. The alcohol had produced its effect, she wasn't hammered but tired, too limp to ask him to leave, to be quite sure she had the right to. The man helped himself to a drink without asking. *He's at home,* she thought. *This bungalow belongs to him, the campsite belongs to him.*

"It's late," she said, all the same.

But he didn't reply. He went up to her and grabbed her by the waist with one hand, caught her face with the other to kiss her on the mouth, full-on. She accepted the kiss, then slowly took a step back. She laughed.

"It's really late, I think it's best if we go to sleep."

His smile told her he didn't believe her for a second, that she also wanted it and he knew it. What could she have done to make him so sure of himself? In the car, she'd wondered if she wanted him. She now realized she was wet. His desire, his powerful grabbing of her waist, the kiss – even if stolen. And yet what she wanted was for him to leave. He lifted her dress, pulled her underwear down abruptly. Maybe she wanted it, after all. It had been quite a while since she'd felt a man's desire – since Noé she's taken less care of her body, and also has less desire. That had an effect on her and she told herself he could wear her down. Besides, it was thanks to him she had a job and a holiday for Noé, so maybe it would be a kind of thank you. No, she didn't really think that, she wasn't really aware of that. If she had been, she'd have reared up in anger and thrown him out, even at the risk of waking Noé, of losing her job. Her reasons were more vague, somewhat alcoholic, guilty – but of what? She let him take her against the sink, her dress at her waist, her underwear around her ankles. It wasn't unpleasant but disappointing. He came quickly and pulled out in time. Then he put his trousers back on and leaned into her to stroke her hair. He could have stroked something else since she hadn't come, but all things considered she preferred him to piss off, she'd do it better herself. He avoided her eyes, said sorry, though she didn't know what he was sorry for. Then he left, closing the door behind him carefully. The water spurting against the stainless-steel sink sounded like a thunderstorm on the roof as she drank, head down, till she was out of breath. She didn't hear the car drive off, but when she stepped out to get a breath of cool air, there was no one there any more.

It could have just been an occupational hazard, an encounter like other similar ones. She'd experienced failed embraces, not very conclusive late-night fucks that leave you distraught or sorry when the details come back in the full light of day. No point in getting all worked up about it, nothing worth remembering if you can put it out of your mind. But the next morning, when she went to work at reception, he appeared in the overheated hut, his face closed, his expression aggressive.

"Get out."

Surprised, she stared, her heart suddenly beating at full speed. It was so astonishing that she couldn't find the words. A sudden nausea rose into her throat, the veins in her neck throbbing like crazy. She finally managed to open her mouth.

"But why?"

The guy shook his head, spittle flew as he put on his act.

"We don't need any prick-teasers like you around here."

"What?"

It was so preposterous, Vanda burst out laughing, but he wasn't deterred. In broad daylight, she saw that he was grey, even tanned.

"Take your kid, pack your bag and get out of my sight."

"Is it your wife?"

The guy turned scarlet and she was afraid he'd hit her. "My wife's a decent woman, a woman with self-respect. You don't even mention her, you hear? You don't even look at her."

"And what am I, you arsehole?"

"A bitch, a prick-teaser. We don't want women like you around here."

Later, when she thought about it again, she was so sorry she hadn't made a scene, smashed everything in the office, roused the customers, the boss's wife and, even if she was sacked, left in the full glory of truth, in an explosion of revenge. Instead, she walked past him, flooding him with her contempt, refraining from spitting at him – honestly, she felt he was capable of hitting her.

Noé was playing outside the hut, crouching in the shade of an umbrella pine. She grabbed him by the hand and dragged him with her. They packed their stuff in a few minutes and pulled their suitcase across the gravel, leaving two deep furrows in their wake. No one stopped to look at the devastating spectacle of their walk across the campsite beneath the blazing sun, no one sensed Vanda's distress, her tears of rage behind the sunglasses. Noé didn't ask any questions. He discreetly pocketed a few teaspoons before saying goodbye to the bungalow. War loot they'd need later, even if he didn't know that there and then.

They headed to the harbour, walking along the motorway in the rasping of the neighbouring bushes, thumbs raised whenever there was a car.

Vanda had less than a hundred euros in her account and there was another fortnight to go before the ferry.

What She's Capable Of

It's a stupid idea but Simon won't let go of it. This time, he didn't take his scooter, preferring to go there on foot. Having his face buffeted by the wind for an hour, casting his gaze into the blue of the coastline, walking from the city centre to the end of the harbour, choosing to walk as close as he can to the sea. It brings back a lot of memories and makes him feel as if he's on holiday. In Paris, he's missed the sea without even realizing it. He's never been to the kid's school but he found the address easily, and he left early enough to get there at least a quarter of an hour before classes end. There are already a few parents there, tapping away on their mobiles, reading the canteen menus displayed on the front gate, saying hello to one another. He hasn't told anyone. Anyway, the only people he's talked to since the other night are the funeral directors' staff regarding payment, and the family notary who explained about the inheritance. He gets the apartment, a better-stocked bank account than he'd imagined. When he talks to Chloé on the phone, they carefully avoid the topic of Noé, even though he hangs over everything. Simon walks through the city, takes familiar paths in spite of himself, finds peace in them. In this city, nothing's urgent, nothing's pressing. What he found so annoying when he left – and what he still criticizes – is doing him good. Even his body relaxes, is freed from constant tension.

Outside the school, the parents smile at him. Finally, the bell, and he's like the others, staring at the gate, champing at the bit. He takes on the role with surprising ease, though it could be like a game. At the same time, isn't that what all the others are also doing? Standing around outside the school, getting a snack ready, uttering end-of-day sentences, forced and repeated ad infinitum – *Did you have a good day? Did you play with your friends during the break? What did you have to eat in the canteen? Have you been good?* The guilt-tripping variants – *Mummy missed you, why did you get your trousers dirty? Where's your jacket?* The unavoidable – *Do you have homework?*

Though Simon has got rid of certain memories, he remembers his mother and the first few times he wished she wouldn't kiss him quite so enthusiastically in front of his schoolmates. What he envies, under all the ready-made phrases parents use to greet their kids, are the love rituals. In the mass, he searches for Noé. It's a structured scramble, the children come out one class at a time, in noisy waves. He watches out for Vanda, slightly dreads her arrival. When he recognizes the child, his body tenses up to call out, but he restrains himself and makes a little hand gesture, with a broad smile and a twinkle in his eye. A neophyte of school leaving time, he thinks he's going to have to argue with the teachers, fight the admin to pick Noé up, prepares his reasons, but the boy pops up next to him.

"Is it you picking me up?"

Simon looks around for disapproving looks from the other adults, expects someone to prevent him from leaving, but nothing.

"Aren't we waiting for your mother?"

"I saw you, so I told the teacher you'll take me home. Maman's often late."

They both walk towards the sea. Simon offers to carry Noé's bag but the child refuses, gives him a smile. He's a nice kid.

When they go down to the beach, the cerulean sea is foaming a little in the distance. The child gallops to the bungalow and unlocks it with his key, a little round key attached to a huge fluffy bird. Simon doesn't go inside. He waits for the child to come back out, and so he reappears, carrying a box of figurines, and gets himself comfortable on the sand.

Simon sits on his jacket, stares at the crests of the waves and follows them until they climax on the sand, amid the seaweed. A slight stomach ache, he fiddles with his mobile, keeps turning on the screen to check if Vanda's replied to his message. He was hoping she'd be here, stupid of him, she's working. He wouldn't want her to worry, but at the same time he's done nothing wrong and he did leave a message, so he's got nothing to blame himself for, and, besides, it was Noé who told his teacher, he has a right to be here.

Even so, when he suddenly sees her rush down the steps and loom up on the beach, she looks like a madwoman and what he reads in her face and body language is a blend of terror and huge anger. Her hair is flying around her head and her face is red from running. Ignoring him, she hurls herself on her son, slaps him hard and grabs him tight in her arms immediately afterwards.

"You never, ever leave without me, do you hear?"

She shouted *never, ever*, the child's mouth is half open, his eyes filled with tears because of the slap. He tries to huddle against her to seek forgiveness and clings to her with the movements of a monkey – a tiny little child even though he's six years old.

As an observer, Simon waits, not at all comfortable but also annoyed, sharp arguments on the tip of his tongue.

"What do you think you're doing, Simon? What do you think? That you can just go pick my son up from school?"

"I sent you a message."

"I don't give a shit about your message."

"I wanted to see my son again."

"Stop that – stop that right now. You've seen him, now you're not going to come and piss us off every couple of days."

"Why?"

Vanda's known this wave of cold before, but not very often. It's always a harbinger of disaster.

Simon wasn't there, he never has been, and she wouldn't have wanted it any other way. When her taut belly distorted the hibiscuses tattooed around her navel, she never thought their relationship had anything to do with it. It was in the past, not an unpleasant past, but simply marginal. Where others hope for or enjoy a hand stroking their forehead and another person comforting them, she had never wanted anything except her solitude. In hospital, she wished she could send away the midwife, the nurses, all those identical-looking smocks that formed an intrusive magma. And yet Vanda had never fed on natural-birth theories of wild women who give birth on all fours in the woods, never wanted to eat her placenta, have a water birth or sing Indian mantras during contractions. No theories shroud her excess of love, her way of acting with her son. Either now or in the beginning.

She may have forgotten the pain of giving birth but she remembers perfectly well how deeply troubled she felt at meeting her child, so small, bent over in frog position, how frighteningly light he was in her belly. Their solitude – the immeasurable pleasure of their solitude.

"You have to leave."

Her voice is menacing, her words a plea. Simon looks at Noé as if waiting for the solution to come from the child, but the child keeps hanging from his mother, a hairy primate with an ambiguous expression. Satisfaction in his eyes, an apologetic half-smile.

"I'll come back, Vanda, whether you like it or not."

Vanda doesn't move, doesn't look at him. It's not clear whether she's heard him or if the backwash has drowned out the man's voice. He's looking at her scornfully, but he's barking up the wrong tree if he thinks it's just a simple power struggle.

"Don't do this."

Simon opens his bag nervously and takes out a colourful album. On the cover, there's a triceratops in relief, with silver varnish on its horns. He puts it down on the sand and addresses only Noé. "It's for you."

With a movement of her hips, she removes the child from Simon's view. Her lip is quivering, but she's not crying. "You don't know what I'm capable of."

Without replying, Simon turns back. He stumbles over the stones, scrapes his soles on the sand, takes the already familiar, wet, narrow steps two by two. His eyes notice the rust on the handrail, pieces of iron stuck in the stone. He's too alone, he needs to talk to someone, and even if Chloé has a strangely remote view of his situation, she's his girlfriend so it counts for something. After all, it's perfectly natural to want to share with her what he's going through, otherwise what's the point, if it's just like being two animals curled up in neighbouring compartments, who communicate only when things are going smoothly. She picks up at the third ring. He blurts it all out and stammers, tries to explain in one go his worries, his anger, and the increasing importance of the child.

"But wait, there's something I don't understand…"

He catches his breath, falls silent to let her continue.

"What are you planning to do, exactly?"

"What do you mean?"

"Do you want to stay and live there?"

"No, but…"

"No? Fuck, Simon, if you're coming back to Paris, what's the point in harassing the woman?"

"I'm not harassing her, I just want to see my kid."

"Stop saying *my kid*, it's preposterous. You've only just discovered he exists. She's the one who produced him, she's the one who wiped his bottom, got up during the night, enrolled him at the nursery."

"Are you giving me the female solidarity spiel?"

"It's the truth. She did it without you, asked nothing of you. Thirty years ago, when a woman complained about a guy carelessly getting her pregnant, she was accused of angling for money or making him marry her to have a place in life. The number of arseholes who had women get themselves pregnant behind their backs, so to speak, is uncountable. And nowadays, when a woman decides to bring up a kid without the help of the guy, it's suddenly an outrage, you're deprived of your fatherhood and all sorts of bullshit."

Chloé doesn't usually use rude words. He noticed she does it when she's angry, and now he finds it repellent, a kind of double whammy. She's probably right, well, in a way, but he doesn't want to listen to her. He wants to be listened to, he wants support. He feels as if his heart and his balls are being crushed, and, shit, now even his girlfriend's having a go at him. He suddenly wonders if he really wants to go back to Paris – the light grabs him by the throat, cuts into his retina, a kind of purplish orange that floods the coast before the sun topples to the other side.

"You're going to lose your job if you don't come back," Chloé adds.

He hears that he's going to lose her, too, and suddenly feels like chucking everything. But he thinks he's a responsible person, not the kind to start from scratch, not the kind who throws the baby out with the bathwater. The kind of man who always complains about being dumped but who does everything to bring this about rather than change things, be the trigger of major changes, the baddie, the one who makes others cry. So he keeps quiet while Chloé carries on, reproaches and requests, stop that bullshit, come back home. She repeats *home* like a mesmerizing spell, as if that could transform their forty-five square metres into a farmhouse with a fireplace. The two of us, the deep carpet, the Chassagne-Montrachet wine they like drinking from large goblets, you and me, no screaming, no plastic toys polluting their environment, no mind-numbing projects that make you think the moon's made of cheese and children are geniuses. It's true that Simon's come to like it, the feeling of being not quite so low down in the food chain and, especially, free, or at least that's what he thought. But now it's all cracking: since his mother's death he's next in line and feels as if everything's tumbling down inside him. Hard as he tries to explain it, it all takes on such a dubious form that Chloé hasn't got a clue, she tries to bring him back to their lives as well as she can, with doses of reason and habit. He does miss her, actually.

"Don't you want to come back here for a few days?" Simon suggests. "I could show you around my old haunts, we didn't even have time to go look at the sea."

"I can't take time from the office just like that."

It seems even more blurred, he can't see a way out, he doesn't know what he wants. He says he'll call back, he needs to think.

He stops for a first beer at the *bar-tabac* at Pointe Rouge. The guys at the bar are commenting on the football and he feels he's a child again, goes over his story in small sips.

What if he did stay here? He's a freelancer anyway, and plenty of Parisians do it. If he took advantage of the move and came back home – that's how he phrases it, come back home, it squeezes his stomach as the thought sinks in. He's always struggling in Paris. To look like what he's not, to keep afloat, to understand the humour, the pace, the priorities. He's the first to make jokes about people in the provinces, so no one can confuse him with that plebeian mob that's content with little and reads the local papers. He's pathetic. A guy pays for the round – there are eight of them in the tiny bar. Simon thinks about the expression in Noé's eyes, his little arms glued around his mother's neck, his hands buried in her witch's mane. He feels like hitting someone, but the guys at the bar seem too friendly for him to pick a fight. Moreover, he thinks it would do him good, but he actually doesn't like punch-ups, he's scared of getting hurt. At the end of the day, he's got too much to lose and then there's the fear. Simon decides to change bars, puts a banknote on the counter for the next round.

"That'll buy three rounds, man. This isn't Paris."

The owner laughs, proud of his remark. He returns two banknotes.

"It's the Parisian's round," he announces.

"I'm local," Simon says defensively.

This need to claim his origins makes him nauseous.

As he walks out, he checks his mobile in the hope of a sign. He's not entirely sure from whom, but from someone who will have thought of him in the past half hour. That obliges him to listen to the messages of his bosses – his *partners*, actually. Freelance my arse, you can't take three days off work without it being the end of the world, he's a one-man band, his family could be ravaged by Ebola and no one would give a shit and they'd still ask him to carry on with the job. He sighs and clenches his teeth as he listens to the recorded messages, tense politeness, threats veiled with diplomacy: he's not the only one around, if he can't stick to a timetable then others will step in.

"Fucking arseholes."

He hasn't sworn so violently in a long time and never at those he works with.

It's obvious he's back, even he's surprised. Things have to change, but he doesn't know how yet. He feels he's growing up, or at least acquiring a form of independence from the world he's always cowered from. Even his going to Paris was just a form of escape, well, perhaps, he's not sure any more, he wonders, he hasn't mourned his mother yet, he doesn't want to go back to work. With the apartment his mother left him and the life insurance, he'd have enough to live on if he moved here. No rent, a nice little sum to set up his own business. It wouldn't be the same in Paris, but why not here? Except that Chloé will never come. And Vanda, will Vanda really let him get to know his son? Simon's anger doesn't know what to focus on. Vanda, Chloé, his partners. Life, death, fate – whatever. He goes to the edge of the sea and walks along the coastline, decides to stop for a drink at every bar he passes to celebrate his metamorphosis – he finally feels like a man, he feels more solid, less translucent since he knows he has a son, or maybe it's the beer, kings gods luck and victory, amen. He's ready to fight now.

One Hundred Per Cent Polyamide

After getting turfed out of the Corsican campsite, the wandering began. The return ferry wasn't for another fortnight and even if Vanda had been able to change their tickets, the hut was let until the end of August. She'd never built strong enough bonds with anyone to consider going to stay with a friend. Even Jimmy and the rest of the gang, whom she'd known for years, remained on the margins of her life. That had drawbacks, but Vanda saw mostly advantages. So, to spare Noé, she presented the situation like a brilliant opportunity, a way for the two of them to have a vacation, and the first night spent out in the open, under a catamaran, was lovely. Even so, rage clung to her, the feeling of injustice and shame, the desire to slaughter that campsite arsehole.

There was still the beauty of the island, the transparent water and the smell of pine trees. Noé, his own smell of grimy little animal covered in salt. During the day, they hung around the beach like ordinary tourists, in swimsuits. Noé was glad to have the chance to be with his mother: she played with him in the water, pretending to be a giant octopus and attacking him with her eight arms. She also agreed to dig tunnels with her hands, dungeon galleries that were more impressive than the actual castle. They used the teaspoons in place of spades. They spent so much time in the sun that after a few days Vanda had become the same colour as her son – a golden-brown that didn't peel.

Even though she didn't want to be indebted to anyone, she had to try a few tactics with the staff of one of the seafront restaurants. Trying to make the owners feel sorry for her and Noé was a dead loss, they'd quickly spotted with suspicion the mother and son who were ogling the customers' plates from their towels on the beach. Sometimes, Vanda would pinch bread from the tables, as she did in the harbour, but the woman who owned the place saw her once and called her a Syrian. Since when was that an insult? It took her a few seconds to react, she was so gobsmacked. On the other hand, they were saved by two waiters, a girl and a guy, so young that, looking at them, she suddenly felt old. She never found out which of the two offered to help her first; maybe it was to please each other that they competed in generosity towards them. It wasn't much, but for Vanda and Noé it was vital: food, when they could, and, after talking to her, they also agreed to give her the key to the toilet block, which was reserved for the customers. Vanda would wait for night-time, for the last members of staff to leave. She'd watch the owner empty the till and go, switch off the lights and lock the restaurant before getting into the passenger seat of the car, her husband behind the wheel. It was often after 2 a.m. by the time silence finally fell on the beach. Then she'd wake up Noé, lying against the hull of a dinghy or a catamaran, and drag him with her. The toilets were adjacent to the restaurant and, on a small duckboard deck, a hosepipe acted as a shower – it was actually for customers to rinse their feet before going to have lunch, but for them it was a chance to wash off the salt that chapped their skin, caused itching, traced white trails down their bodies. The water was cold and Noé would cry as he stood shivering, whining to escape from this harsh awakening. Vanda had noticed that the first few litres of water were still warm thanks to the daytime heat on the hosepipe, but that didn't last. She tried to be as quick as she could to prevent Noé from getting ill. Even though the nights in Corsica were often mild, the early mornings would catch them unawares, a humid chill that made them shiver before the sun was up, baking the surroundings.

She found Noé had successfully adapted to the situation, though he clung to her even more whenever he could, in the water or on the sand – his body had to be joined to his mother's in some way or other, and when he couldn't stick to her he'd take her hand and couldn't bear her disappearing even for a few minutes. She drew no conclusions from this. She needed him as much as he needed her, there was no doubt about that. Besides, she had no choice.

It was more complicated when it came to getting him to sleep. Noé had left his cuddly toy at the campsite and after much thinking she decided it must have fallen in the small garden at the back of the bungalow – the last time she'd seen her son holding it was when she was snatching their washing, all wrinkled from the sun, off the line in a rush to stuff it in their suitcase. The suitcase she was now hiding under the hull of a turned-over Optimist, its torn fibreglass explaining why it had been abandoned.

Every night, Noé would grow tense, kneading handfuls of his T-shirt, missing his cuddly toy. The only way Vanda had found to help him fall asleep was to let him stroke her hair. He was doing it increasingly often even when it wasn't night-time, calming down while digging his fingers into her thick mane, his other hand – or at least his thumb – in his mouth.

Sometimes, he'd lean with his back against her belly as she sat facing the sea. At the time when tourists put away their beach equipment, when groups of teenagers heaved boats onto the sand, rolled up the sails and chased after one another after putting on their clothes over their swimsuits, she and Noé would turn into a statue. A single form for two bodies, their faces motionless, straining towards the sea and the evening lights, Vanda's arms wrapped around her son's warm tummy.

She didn't want to get involved with anyone. She didn't like the mothers who caked their children with sun cream and had their straw-hatted heads in their books. To be honest, she didn't like the whole world, the whole world could have disappeared, only her son and she were important. She would sometimes whisper to him, "You and me, Limpet, against the world."

After much thinking, an idea had taken shape in Vanda's head: to go back to the campsite and get the cuddly toy, triumphantly bring the beloved item back to Noé. Despite the fear of bumping into the arsehole, she made up her mind.

One night, she left the child asleep under the Optimist, the hull slightly raised and propped up by a large stone, and went to the campsite through the pine wood. There were sounds in the undergrowth but the moon lit the path well – fifteen minutes on foot, no more. Her heart beat fast as soon as she made out the first tent pitches, the central alley, then, as she approached in the shadows, the tea lights hanging from the convenience shop-café, in the heart of the campsite. There were still people on the terrace. She heard voices, laughter, the chords of an old Britney Spears song every time someone opened the door to come out. She casually walked to the patch with the bungalows, spotted the one where she'd stayed with Noé. Lights off, no car parked outside, no washing hanging, no beach towels drying. Vanda approached, gathered her hair on one side and plaited it roughly without tying it. It was just a matter of not getting it caught everywhere as she rummaged at the back of the bungalow, where downy oaks stretched their branches at human height. It didn't take her long to find the chewed-up triceratops, fallen on the edge of the wall, and she pounced on it, overjoyed at the prospect of Noé's happiness when he was reunited with it. Then, standing in the dark, holding the cuddly toy tight against her and her heart beating with fear and anger, Vanda decided to go into the bungalow. Perhaps because this little haven had been snatched away from them unfairly, so it was sort of still their home. Or perhaps, deep down, she was already considering revenge. The latch resisted and she forced it with a stone. It was hellishly hot inside, as is always the case with little plasterboard houses that turn into an oven as soon as the sun shines and barely cool down at night when you leave the windows open. The windows were shut, no doubt had been since they'd left. She stood motionless in the tiny kitchen for a moment, her bum against the sink, she lit a cigarette. She hasn't really thought about it, but if it had to be done all over again, she'd do it: set fire to the blankets, all the blankets, with her Moor's head Corsica lighter. Methodically, every corner of the blankets, then the pillows, the two mattresses.

She checked that things caught fire properly, that it wouldn't go out pathetically and leave her stranded with her hatred. No, out of the question. It had to be a blaze, she had to make him pay for this anxiety-ridden fortnight, this loneliness of being just the two of them, without a penny, their homeless-style holiday. She needed revenge for Noé's fitful sleep as he rolled in the sand like a fennec fox, his eyes irritated by the salt, the waiting for the boat, waiting too long. She was suddenly afraid that the smoke would stifle the fire, so she opened the windows to create a draught, and that really worked a treat. Only the mattresses took a while to catch fire: they were smoking a lot but were eaten away at rather than blazed. That's when she saw the curtains, a revolting bright purple, one hundred per cent polyamide, you can't get any more flammable than that. They burned immediately and she left, her T-shirt over her nose, ran away to watch from a distance. It was perfect, a real giant torch, wood, synthetic and plasterboard were burning beautifully. She held the triceratops tight in one hand, her cigarette still in the other, and ended up crushing the stub with her heel before it burned her fingers. The noise grew into a roar, the sound of small explosions was coming from inside, and the blaze lit up the surroundings. People started coming out of the neighbouring bungalows, screams, bodies crowding together to watch or else take out a mobile, call the firefighters. She didn't wait to see the campsite owner before she left – the image of the bungalow on fire was enough for her revenge. She'd been walking through the pine wood for five minutes when she heard the fire engine's siren in the distance. Her step became a skip, like that of a deer. She was still singing "Toxic" to herself when she reached the beach.

The evening before their departure, Vanda decided to blow her last euros and treat them to a meal at the beach restaurant. The waitress winked at her, surprised to see them sitting at a table, but glad to take their order. Only it wasn't her but the owner who reappeared with their food. He first placed the huge plate of fries in front of Noé before sliding a board of fine cured meats before Vanda.

"I didn't order this," she said, with the softness of a moray eel.

"I know," the large man replied before pulling up a chair. "May I?"

Vanda didn't answer, tense from head to toe. She took comfort from seeing her son attacking the fries with the smile of a malnourished child. It hurt her in her belly, but also gave her immediate joy to see her boy so radiant.

"Go on, try it, it's delicious."

She picked a piece of pancetta with her fingers, then two: the stuff melted in your mouth, an orgasm for the taste buds, it actually made her cheeks quiver, it made a change from tuna-and-tomato sandwiches crunchy with sand. It's true that they'd got a fair number of cold dishes thanks to the waiters but not regularly and, above all, they were impossible to keep; anything they didn't eat, they had to throw away.

"My family makes them."

"Compliment them for me," she managed to say between mouthfuls.

"And it's on us."

He looked super glad to see her eat with such appetite. So she slowed down. What was this *on us* business? – she went on alert. He stretched his legs under the table and his foot hit the suitcase.

"Are you leaving?"

"Yes, tomorrow morning."

"I hope you won't keep too bad a memory of Corsica."

"What do you mean?"

"I don't know what happened to you before you ended up here, but I'm sorry you had to stay on the beach like that. And with a child."

A bit too late to worry about that. After ignoring them for two weeks. Vanda tore a piece of bread, stuffed a huge chunk of figatellu into it and resumed her devouring conspicuously. He sighed, looking embarrassed.

"You look a bit odd, people aren't used to it."

"Odd?"

"Your tattoos and stuff."

She'd have liked to snigger but she was too upset.

"It's actually quite pretty but we're not used to it, you see. Especially on a woman."

What was he trying to do, exactly? Was he coming on to her or was it his way of taking the piss? She'd have liked to bite but above all she wanted to cry, and she couldn't help being grateful for the cured meats. She was scared it would turn sour before she'd finished her board.

"Can I have some more?"

Noé was smiling, his plate cleaned out except for the grains of salt and swirls of ketchup scraped on the bottom.

"Of course, wait."

The owner called the waitress and leaned towards Noé. "Would you also like a burger?"

The kid nodded like mad, his eyes glistening.

The waitress left with the plate and a triumphant smile.

"What are you doing, exactly? I haven't got the money to pay for all this and you know it."

"It's my daughter."

"What?"

"The waitress is my daughter. The one who's been giving you food in Tupperware for two weeks. The one who slipped you the keys to the toilets – with my permission, naturally."

"Oh, shit."

"My wife wasn't very happy about it, she's scared of strangers. At first, she sulked. But the peach-scented soap by the sink, that was her idea."

If the whole family were in on it, he couldn't have expected anything in return, like a blow job in the toilet. He just needed her gratitude; being a benefactor without an audience loses some of its worth. Unless you're some kind of saint, everybody likes gratitude.

"Well, thank you, then."

"I wanted to apologize for not helping you sooner. But, you understand, with all the things you see. Even just in the campsite up the road, they had a fire this weekend and apparently it was arson, they say."

Vanda tensed up again, all her saliva dried up. She stared at the man to find out more, but he beamed a large smile as he watched his daughter return with a full plate for Noé.

"And what about you? What will you have after the cured meats? Some chicken? A filet mignon?"

"Frankly, if you could give me the same again, that would be brilliant."

The man looked delighted that his family's cured meats were such a hit. He grabbed his daughter by the arms and said, "And bring us a little Clos Canarelli, please? And a glass."

It was a lovely evening. Noé fell asleep on his mother's lap, full and exhausted, after a white-chocolate Magnum. The restaurant owner didn't let her pay and offered to drop them off at the harbour the following morning. It made the final hours of their stay less bitter than the rest of it, and when Vanda and Noé remember that summer together, this last meal has a special place in their recollections.

But for Vanda, and Vanda alone, the smell of the fire and the sound of the blaze are still her best memories. The kind that make her stand straight, and strong.

Bloody Hell, This Is France

When Vanda comes out of the metro, she emerges in the middle of an already dense crowd, a maelstrom of banners, singing and chanting of slogans. She used to like crowds, a way of getting lost in the great whole, anonymous. And also after living in a village, getting lost in numbers had something intoxicating about it. Back in the days when she had a go at art college, she attended a few demonstrations with people from her class, but mainly illegal demos, artistic events and blockades. It was fierce, funny, sometimes violent, but a contained, framed violence – like playing cat and mouse. Naturally, there was a bit of roughing up at the end, and the wilder ones would end up in prison. From what she's heard in the past few months, what's going on now is something else. No children around her, no old people, but tense faces, orders to retreat, phone numbers of specialist lawyers exchanged. She passes groups, trade unions and not, fluorescent yellow and red and black, blends: she doesn't quite understand what's so amazing about them. Over there, a group of cleaning ladies exploited by a big hotel, they've been striking for weeks – as you can tell from their banner, something confirmed by their tired, worried faces. Over here, a housing committee born out of the collapse, the advanced age of buildings, poorly rehoused families. Vanda slowly walks through the crowd, like an ingredient added to a cake mixture. She hasn't enjoyed this for quite a while, preferring solitude, a swim in the sea, to the headiness of crowds. The only kinds of multitude she still enjoys are at concerts and in bars. Bars especially, because even at concerts she has some trouble – and it's got worse since Bataclan. Even in the provinces, the massacre caused a trauma. She can no longer hear a firecracker without jumping, suspecting death behind every explosion.

A hand squeezes her arm and pulls her back.

"Vanda, you came! We're down there, next to the green truck."

Thierry drags her along and she sees her colleagues from the hospital, a small crowd glued to the truck, which is churning out repetitive music that's supposed to be rousing. And yet there's nothing joyous about this gathering that's crying out for a joint struggle, but which is surrounded increasingly heavily by hundreds of riot police in helmets. The demonstration hasn't even started yet. Some women are here for the first time. Samia smiles, looking totally lost in this universe she's discovering. She never comes into the city centre, not even at the week-end. She prefers to go to the Grand Littoral shopping centre, there's always room to park and everything she needs. She came once or twice to discover the shopping streets, but she doesn't really like the city centre, it's a bit frightening for her. There are other cleaning ladies here, surprised at sharing this march with nurses, carers and teachers. There are even two psychologists from the child psychiatry service and a doctor from Wing 12. It looks like a retirement leaving do, the only time the professions really get to mix.

"Don't go far, let's all stay together as much as possible, OK? Last time it really went tits up and the people in yellow get gassed every Saturday. So no more silly games – if things start heating up, we buzz off."

Samia nods, eyes staring – shit, all these precautions scare the hell out of you, it's just a demonstration to say they don't agree with the management reshuffle at the hospital, or with the public services cuts, or with the increase in temporary contracts instead of giving workers permanent ones. Vanda puts a hand on her shoulder.

"Don't worry, we're better off here than cleaning rooms."

That makes Samia smile but she doesn't worry any less.

"I hope this isn't going to get us sacked. Can you imagine? What will I do if they sack me?"

Vanda doesn't reply but is also imagining it. That would be really shitty. The temping agency would no doubt find her something else, in a worse set-up, and maybe even further away, now her car's out of action. She'd rather not think about it too much. It's frightening, but that's not a reason to kowtow.

The demonstration gradually thins out and goes up the wide avenue. Behind them, the merchant seamen are yelling. They refused to load weapons for Saudi Arabia, French weapons destined to kill people in Yemen.

"I can't see the connection," Samia says.

"Joint struggle," Thierry answers. He looks like a combatant with that devoted expression – it makes Vanda smile, also irritates her a little. But after all he's right, and this blend of inconsequential beings ready to shout in the street is a reminder: they have names, jobs, ethics, they're a legion despite the deafening silence of an increasingly unfair power.

It begins at the level of Cours Lieutaud. At first, she hears shouts, then the crowd suddenly ebbs back towards Canebière. She steps back to avoid the scramble, but the density becomes a solid mass and bodies compress around her. Shots are fired and grenades roll, giving out thick, toxic, unbearable smoke. Actual curtains of tear gas rise, compact, and the shouts become screams. The riot police that have surrounded them in rows since the beginning of the march start hitting every demonstrator within reach indiscriminately. People choke and try to run away from the tangle, but the streets leading off the road are blocked by police cars, so jaws clench. More shooting, screams of pain. Riot police, the anti-crime squad, Vanda can't tell the difference and they're all hitting and shooting with equal violence, anyway. She's heard testimonies about gouged eyes and hands torn off in the most total indifference – a mark of a bewildering denial. But knowing about it and experiencing it isn't the same thing. Next to her, Samia is out of breath from shrieking, clinging to every moving body. Thierry's disappeared, so has the driver of the union truck. Only the music hasn't stopped, and it's like the soundtrack of a film, except that the violence is real, and Keny Arkana's anger doesn't calm anyone down. Her voice flies over the carnage, beats to the rhythm of the blows.

During a lull, Vanda rushes between two policemen too busy to see her and manages to glue herself to the wall behind them. There are scenes of slaughter, of unimaginable violence everywhere. The demonstrators run and scream, cornered and struck by the police. Vanda has trouble breathing, feels anxiety rising and paralysing her, when Thierry appears, grabs her by the arm and drags her into a street in Noailles. Panicking, other demonstrators escape around them like wild animals chased by a forest fire. But the police are everywhere, hunting demonstrators even down the alleys, catching them and hitting them. Even when they're on the ground, curled up, even unconscious. And no black hoods, militants ready to tackle them. You can hear a few outbursts of unimaginative insults, many cries of distress. At the corner of a square, in the heart of the district, a dozen policemen are beating up a young woman on the ground. Her head's cracked, she's unconscious and blood is gushing onto the road. Vanda is frozen, unable to run. The police keep kicking the young woman when a guy comes hurtling and shouting, "I'm a doctor, let me through!"

But the police turn around and form a wall. They surround him and advance to make him step back.

"Something has to be done for her, you can see she's in a really bad state."

"Fuck off!"

"Get lost!"

"We said get lost!"

The man stands with his mouth half open, in total disbelief that they won't let him go near, that the young woman's head keeps bleeding and no one's taking her to hospital. She has long hair, caked in blood, her short, patterned dress has ridden up above her thighs, her tights are torn. The doctor repeats on a loop, like an idiot, "What kind of world do you live in? In what kind of world do you leave people to die after beating them to death? Bloody hell, this is France!"

His cries have the power to irritate the police even more. Vanda's terrified – nausea rises in her throat, she feels her legs turn to jelly, her breath getting shorter and shorter. Thierry stamps, panicking. "Let's go, Vanda, shit, let's go."

As one of the policemen approaches her, truncheon in hand, her legs suddenly unblock and she starts to run. She's never run this fast. She's reassured by Thierry's breath, his haphazard strides next to her. Sometimes, he overtakes her and that helps her speed up. They cut across the streets as best they can, reach the mass of tourists who haven't seen anything, slalom between the strollers who look increasingly unconcerned, so they allow themselves to slow down, look back. No more police. People around them are taking a walk, a couple of teenagers are kissing. A man is playing a barrel organ, his cap upside down on the flagstones. Distraught, they look at each other. Thierry shakes his head.

"It's insane."

Vanda's hands are shaking, she struggles to catch her breath. They don't speak to each other, drift like zombies, are startled by any loud noise. Neither of them is going back to the demonstration. Gradually, the people who've escaped the blows will run away and get into a car, a bus, a bar. The others will go to hospital to try and explain about the attack, the violence, get treated. Some doctors will listen, others won't. And then there'll be all the ones who'll spend the night in jail, weep so they can make a phone call, some to an ex-wife so she picks up the kids from school, some to a relative so they don't worry, to a boyfriend or girlfriend who won't be able to understand how this happened, how you can end up in a police station if you haven't done anything wrong. Then those who still have their legs, their eyes, their hands, and who've managed to hide in one of the city's crevices, will come back out after nightfall. They won't feel like going home. They'll be filled with so much rage that they'll burn anything they find, stack up tyres, bins, and set them on fire. They may not have been wearing hoods earlier, but they will now.

As for Vanda, all she wants is to go back to Noé's skin and the protection of their hut. They might as well wait for the end of the world there. She shouldn't be late, she thinks, and picks up the pace. She can't get the image of the bloodied young woman out of her mind. She slowly catches her breath, clings to Thierry's arm.

"What's this about a trial with Magalie?"

The question popped out, the question she'd been wanting to ask for a long time. But now she asks it as if it's urgent, or as a way of not talking about what they've just been through.

"Have you been following the Télécom issue?"

Yes, Vanda's been following, the start of the trial against France Télécom managers, their shitty policies of pushing people out, *through the door or the window*, harassing workers until they snapped and ten or so committed suicide. She read an article in which one of the managers was saying he didn't understand what they were accusing him of. He talked about the suicides as if it were a fashion trend.

She drags Thierry to a quiet spot, hoping to catch a bus without needing to return to the harbour.

"And what about Magalie?"

"That's when she lost it. She and her husband worked at France Télécom. He hanged himself in the office. She wasn't doing well either and after that she went off the rails."

A cold shiver goes up Vanda's back.

She can't think of anything to say, thinks about Magalie's blank eyes, pictures her before, in a normal life. She's no longer the patient in pyjamas, who lets her toenails grow and rocks in a plastic garden chair, smears her period blood on her bedroom walls, laughs like a hyena, for no reason. She wears a suit, or fitted jeans, maybe high heels, and her hair is done.

"And what will she do when she leaves the hospital, when she's better?"

"It's complicated. As you can imagine, she's lost all her friends. I know she has a sister who takes her in. And she also tries to see her daughter sometimes. She has a twelve- or thirteen-year-old kid, or thereabouts."

"Fucking hell."

"Yep, it's tough. We're not worth a penny. That's not even cynicism, it goes beyond that." Thierry's voice falters on those final words.

Vanda needs to be with Noé right away. She's shaken violently by this and is ready to cross another wall of tear gas just so she can reduce the space between herself and her son. She squeezes Thierry's arm without managing a smile, thanks him for having been there. And, abandoning the idea of a bus, Vanda starts running again, a mad sprint on the edge of the harbour, towards the cliff road. If she catches the bus, so much the better – if not, she can keep running. The sea to her right, Tangier on the other side. At the end of the road, there's her son.

She noticed Thierry's *we* that puts them on the same side as Magalie. They're so disposable, they're all going to end up the same way. She's known this for a long time, that she's worth nothing or not much. She discovered it very early on, since her mother wasn't exactly worth a huge amount. And it gets worse at every meeting at the temping agency, every time the internet cuts off just while she's filling in an endless form to apply for housing assistance. It continues when her money hasn't cleared in time for even a minor school outing and the teachers sigh with anger, when poor people's houses collapse while the city centre is redesigned to look like a film set. Hatred blends with fear – Vanda feels on the brink of an explosion, on the very edge. Let them drop dead. Let their cynical smiles be cut wider with a knife. Let them choke on their contempt, stuff their millions up their arses and drop dead.

A Room of Your Own

He's tried calling Vanda several times but keeps getting her voicemail. She must have switched off her mobile while at work. Simon's decided he won't let go. It's the result of his bar crawl the other night. Drinking brings out priorities, he kept telling himself, increasingly drunk as he left one bar to move on to another. But the bistros on the beach smell of emptiness, as well as coarse albeit gilded youth. You have to drink mojitos to fit in, so he caught a bus back to the city centre and ended up at the Bar de la Plaine for a large part of the night. There, no one was likely to offer him some crap with a pink umbrella stuck in it or charge him the price of a cocktail for a beer. Roadworks had drilled holes in the street, a wall was shielding the diggers in the legendary square, the heart of the district, the nerve centre of the city for a certain category of people – to which he'd belonged for a long time. On the surrounding wall, graffiti, poems and photos were screaming the residents' anger. On a rounded corner, in dark letters: *Zineb Redouane, murdered by the police: neither forget nor forgive.* He did a Google search to see who she was, gritted his teeth as he read the article and concentrated on not thinking about her any more.

At the Bar de la Plaine, he bumped into Greg, and Greg helped him see things clearly. He wasn't really clear, actually, having started on aniseed *mauresques bassines* a while back. Simon hadn't seen Greg for over ten years. They'd stopped hanging out after high school. When Simon started at art college, Greg took over his uncle's garage. He still works there, the uncle died of a brain tumour, so now he's managing the three employees and the apprentices. They were glad to see each other, but at the same time they no longer knew one another, a bit like giving a warm welcome to a stranger. They talked about the three or four mates they had in common, slagged off Girard, the bastard principal they both had, who gave them a hard time – oh, how they got back at him, how they laughed. Then Greg told Simon at length about his divorce, his ex-wife who does all she can to fleece him like a sheep. About the children he doesn't get to see often enough, because of work and that bitch, you work your arse off to support a family and Madam's whims – and pow! Life's a bitch and women are sluts. Simon didn't agree with the whole tirade, but Greg's confessions prompted him to start talking, too, and didn't it feel fucking good. It was easier than with Chloé – Greg's still a good guy even years later, ready to agree with Simon on everything. Unconditional support, a male bastion. They kept the rounds going in time with their respective complaints, the more insignificant, the more vindictive. And Greg told him over and over again, "It's up to you to decide, it's your fucking son! You're not going to let your ex deprive you of your son."

*

Simon massages the back of his neck, seals a box marked *Maman's Stuff, basement,* with duct tape. He can't make himself throw the lot out. Writing *Maman* with the marker, he has a lump in his throat.

Drinking brings out the priorities and his son is a priority, he's sure of it. He feels he's developing consistency. Enough to gear himself up to empty his mother's apartment, sort, fold, give away or chuck. To call Vanda every hour to put pressure on her, so she doesn't even for a second imagine he's going to give up. To start imagining a new place for his son. A bedroom. A child's bedroom.

He's chosen his old bedroom because of the golden light that floods in as soon as it's morning. He didn't spend hours stacking up Lego pieces in this room he inhabited rather late, as a teenager. Before that, he was living in an old, working-class area, alone with his mother. Back then, the district still smelled of grilled sardines, of grass smoked beneath their windows, of poverty. It was grubby and the police didn't hang around there. Even the little tourist train got attacked by the local Indians, kids fed up with being gawped at like circus animals whenever the loudspeaker announced: *the district of the first Italian immigrants, one of the city's most working-class areas.* The time for Italians was over – now there were still a few Corsicans and mostly Arabs. The new Indians refused to be allocated to a reservation. But that didn't stop regentrification, years later, the creation of artisan boutiques for tourists, the rise in rents, like everywhere else.

Simon remembers that on 15 August, the procession with the Virgin Mary would parade beneath their windows – puffs of incense wafting into the living room, men strapped with ropes, prayers. He wasn't a believer but it was fascinating, a kind of solemn carnival, a journey back in time. Years later, he went to Andalusia during Holy Week and recognized that childhood feeling, the impression of witnessing secret rituals full of a meaning that escaped him. There was also the feast of Eid and the weeks of Ramadan, during which the streets would fill with stalls heaped with honey cakes. Incense and honey are like Proust's madeleine to him, and all he has to do is walk into a church, even though he's not baptized, to immediately find himself on a cobbled street in the Cordelles, or eat angel hair to escape to Montée des Accoules, be back with his friends in the middle of a large well of light disrupted by washing swaying from the windows.

Childhood was quite fun. He doesn't remember their being deprived of anything whatsoever, he and his mother. She was a teacher and taught literacy at the community centre on Wednesdays. Their apartment was small, under the roof. In the summer, it was like the inside of an oven: his mother would put a fan in every room to make the hot air circulate. She met his stepfather at the community centre. He ran integration programmes, but sat behind a desk, talked of second chances with his shirt tucked into his trousers. He didn't have an accent. Simon knows he's always been unfair to his stepfather. Even now, he thinks about him with extreme unkindness and unfairness. And yet he was a nice guy, and he made many efforts to tame this recalcitrant child who wanted nothing to change, to keep his mother all to himself past the appropriate age. His arrival in their lives disrupted certain rituals but that was natural. And yet the only child carried on kicking and screaming to stay at the centre of the world, tirelessly rejecting the stepfather's overtures, convinced he'd been robbed of something. Adolescence was carnage.

In spite of everything, Simon had maintained acceptable grades at school, and art college had opened the doors to other possible worlds. He liked photography, created collages that attracted a fair amount of praise, hung around with inspired people. But he quickly realized that he needed precision and obligations, that he required concrete issues, so he'd enrolled at graphic art school. Moreover, Simon wanted to be taken seriously. An artist, that's not serious. There was always someone to remind you of that. And to be taken seriously, you also had to leave, go up to Paris, earn your stripes and settle down. This place wasn't serious, never, no matter what you did to appear so. Theatre, painting, architecture, graphic design. No use. And the worst was that there was some truth in it. What's really serious here is not to miss the aperitif hour.

And yet it's a tragic city where the toothless, the malnourished, the ugly, the small survive. Chloé wasn't wrong. You can die in the sun like anywhere else, you can suffer under the blue sky, but people will always struggle to believe it. They'll think about the summer beaches and not hear the song of the dead, of the thousands of immigrants who've arrived in waves from all over the Mediterranean, from good-time worshippers to the rescue ship *Aquarius*. Even if you don't venture to the north of the city, even if you don't look left when you climb up to the Sormiou hills, it's hard to skirt the prison walls and dive into the sea from the arid heights. Even Simon often chose to turn away, count the beers on the back seat, point out to his girlfriends the size of the maritime pines and the tears of sap that make them untouchable, the multitude of prickly pears, their small flowers set among the thorns.

Simon's back in his city and he can't tell if it's doing him any good. He stacks the boxes for the basement by the front door, goes back to the now empty room, already pictures a child's bed, turns his face to the window: the trees in the park form a green horizon, rare in town. He wonders if Noé would like to go and play there. Simon doesn't envisage taking his son trudging in the hills. He doesn't like the countryside. He went hiking with his friends, girlfriends especially, but it always annoyed him. The mosquitoes when evening falls, the sticky heat as soon as it's morning, which spoils sleeping in your sleeping bag, the sore back, the damp clothes – nobody minded except him. Returning to the city felt like salvation. And the closure of the *calanques* in the summer is a blessing. No more rucksacks on scorching paths, no more trying to fuck on rocky ground, getting tangled up in sweaty sleeping bags. At the same time, the blue horizon, tone on tone, is, admittedly, priceless. Drinking brings out priorities and the blue is a priority, he'd forgotten that, or simply hadn't fully realized it: for that he needed to leave and come back.

So the nearby park will be, he imagines, for birthday teas. Blank walls to cover with pictures, dinosaurs, Pokémon, drawings.

He wonders how things would have turned out if he'd been here. If he'd seen Vanda's belly grow month after month. If he'd seen his son from birth, red and wrinkled, heard his first cry. She robbed him of that and of all the firsts of early childhood – he lists them to fuel his conviction. A new-father litany: the first smiles, the tentative steps, the first day at school. He forgets the sleepless nights, the fear, the constraints. He listens to himself saying he would have been there, attentive and committed. That he's going to catch up on all this lost time.

Vanda isn't going to screw him – it's his fucking son.

This Is My Home

"How much do you need?"

"It's just for the car, I'll pay you back."

"No need."

Vanda scowls. She cracked. She keeps telling herself she didn't have a choice, Simon kindly offered and she really needs that car. Besides, he's got money and she hasn't. If she loses her job, she'll really be in the shit. Since her car died, she's been late twice. Between being late and the strike, she's on probation. Simon hands her four large, folded banknotes, she stuffs them into the pocket of her jeans, nice and deep. By agreeing to come, these fucking repairs are costing her even more, but it's too late to back out, the food's about to be served.

"I met an old high-school mate who has a garage, I'll give you his address if you like, I'm sure if you mention me he'll do a good job."

The view is sublime. Simon picked the restaurant. When Vanda agreed to see him again, he wanted it to be all nice: the terrace overlooks the sea, between Catalans and Malmousque. Blue as far as the eye can see and rocks down below. From here, they can't hear the noise of cars on the cliff road a few metres above them, only the backwash and the wind. Noé is bored, leans over the railing.

"Shit, get down from there, I said get down!"

Vanda's voice is rough, she yanks him down, plonks him in his chair.

"Gently… he's curious, it's natural."

She holds back the insults that rush straight up to her throat, looks at the arsehole and his calculated kindness, his sly approach. He calls her too often, won't make up his mind to leave, takes up a lot of room. When the waiter puts the plates down in front of them, she takes advantage and focuses on her son again, cuts his burger into tiny pieces, attacks the soft meat as if it were something else.

"Can't you cut your own meat, big guy?"

That's too much. Without even turning her head, Vanda knocks the nearest glass of wine with the back of her hand. The liquid runs down the table and Simon has to leap back to limit the damage.

"You're crazy! What did you do that for?"

"Wasn't on purpose."

"Are you kidding me?"

He hesitates, at the same time he's not sure, it was all very quick. But there's her expression, right there, her eyes sticking into his, like forks.

"I can't afford to kid. But I'd quite like you to stop it with your shitty remarks, anyway. He's my son, I've been raising him for six years, I didn't ask for your opinion."

"I'm entitled to ask a question."

"No. Actually, no, so stop it with your questions. I don't even know why I agreed to come, fucking hell."

She buries her face in her hands, takes a deep breath, Noé eats his fries drowned in ketchup, listens attentively to the exchange.

"So you can get money off me?"

"Yeah, actually, that's exactly it. Happy now? I work my arse off to pay the rent, I've had my wages cut, which aren't exactly high, and I don't even know if I'm going to be kept on."

"I didn't know."

"Things haven't changed much, have they? Even ten years ago, you were the one who paid when we went out. Does it make you feel good? Do you feel all strong and manly?"

"Why wouldn't they want to keep you on?"

"Because I went on strike. And it seems it's actually my fault the others did, too."

It's the HR manager who told her unofficially, convinced that if Samia and the others dared get involved, then it was bound to be because of loudmouths like her. And yet she always keeps her mouth shut at work. Except that she never lowers her eyes.

"I like helping you."

She suddenly screams, a cry that's at the same time loud and contained, kicks the base of the table. Noé stiffens, hunches and pushes the fries away with his fingertips. The people around turn towards them, then away from the scene, going back to their business and their moules marinières before they get cold. Simon's astounded, his steak is bleeding but it doesn't occur to him to get stuck into it. He's scared, guesses without knowing it for a fact that Vanda's capable of lashing out even harder than he imagined.

"Do you think I give a shit that you like it? Do you think it's nice for me to have to accept your money?"

"Things could be different, you know."

Simon's shaking inside, Vanda's whisper is like a slap: "And how would you like things to be different, exactly? You want us to become a family? If you believe that then you're totally off your head. You and I don't even know each other. I was nice enough to introduce Noé to you and now you've been hanging around here for several weeks. If I thought you'd take root here, I wouldn't have done it."

As the words come out, her arms wave about, her powerlessness in twists of the wrists, fingers extending and clasping emptiness, then fiddling with a fork. Simon watches her without warmth: he has steeled himself.

"And what about you, Noé? What do you think?"

The little boy's kept his head down, a lock of hair conceals his large, rabbit-in-the-headlights eyes.

"You can't ask him that, he's six years old."

"So? Maybe he wants to get to know me and see his new room."

Vanda's hand tightens around the fork, her knuckles white from the pressure. Her powerlessness turns to rage.

"His what?"

"His new room."

"I thought you were going back to Paris. When are you leaving, exactly?"

The time Simon takes to reply feels like an infinity.

Vanda's heart is turning inside out with anxiety, is beating at an incredible speed.

"I think I'll stay."

It falls like a pebble on the plates, the sauce curdles, nothing else will go down Vanda's throat, except the wine, which she swallows in a large gulp, her hand shaking.

"No, you're not staying."

"That's actually not your decision. This is my home."

Simon's sending signals to Noé, affectionate smiles and even a wink. The kid is stupefied, his eyes increasingly glued to his mother, stalking her reactions. He can feel her suffering and that scares him, so, in a charged and angry movement against the one who's causing all this upset, he clings to his mother, tries to climb clumsily on her lap. She pushes him away gently.

"Eat your fries, my Limpet, don't worry. He's not going to take you far away from me, I'm here."

"He's worried about your reaction, not about me."

"You think you know him? Really?"

"Listen, I'm doing my best, but let me make it clear: he's my son and I have rights. I want to acknowledge this kid, whether you like it or not. After that, it'll be up to the judge, and given your situation and the dump you make him live in, I'm not sure that…"

He stops here, aware he's gone too far. But she needs a shock to understand, damn it, she can't just do whatever she wants. As shocks go, this one looks like a well-aimed uppercut. Vanda is numbed and her confusion turns to blind rage. Her eyes wander and follow the flying seagulls. It looks as though she's switched off. The child doesn't take his eyes off her, his little hand seeks hers, the fries no longer have any taste, they're cold anyway, and cold fries are disgusting. Simon searches for words, he'd like to stall now it's got complicated, he doesn't like conflict, he's hopeless in a fight, what he'd like is for everything to happen gently, oh, how he wants it. It's all got screwed up.

Vanda gets up, neither violent nor serene – with deliberate slowness so she can contain her simmering rage. She grabs her bag, Noé's hand in hers.

"You can't leave just like this, you two haven't even eaten."

"I'm not hungry any more. Neither is Noé. You've ruined our appetite."

She goes, then turns, walks straight back to Simon so he worries she's going to hit him, you never know with her.

"I'm keeping the money. For you, it's a detail, for me, it's essential."

Simon refrains from answering. He watches her walk away again, the kid at the end of her flower-patterned arm. After she disappears, his eyes fall back on the plates full of cold food, like a mass grave he ordered. He finds it unfair, and he's not hungry any more either.

What Her Mother Didn't Know

The boy was a year older than her. He had a jutting chin and a crooked tooth, little eyes with which he squinted to look fierce. Blue eyes, rather nice, and a blond's skin that turned red as soon as he was embarrassed. She can't remember his name. But she remembers him because you always remember the first times. The first time she fought with her fists, the first time that she struck to hurt, that she made an opponent bleed.

"Your mother sleeps with all the men."

The cruelty of small villages where people know everything, the conformism of children who will always brandish moral rules. In the beginning, a child isn't aware of differences, is ready to welcome another. Bullshit, as Vanda realized very early on. Besides, she, too, would have preferred her mother to conform to what was expected of a woman on her own. Tolerance is something you learn. Or not.

And yet she stood up for her mother so often, before the silence. Before scurrying off, burning bridges, as they say, before going far away. Did she know what Vanda had to put up with?

That day, she'd beaten the creep up, washed away the insult, saved her honour, as if her mother's virtues would come back out intact thanks to this thrashing. She didn't know how far they respected the good old rules of traditional duelling over there, the premise that the winner, whose hand is guided by God, is always right. The worst was that she quite liked this kid, even more than just liked, she'd kissed him on the mouth during a school outing the year before; hiding in the ferns, they'd used their tongues just like in films.

After she'd administered her first punch and blood had smeared his cheek, dripping from his nostril to his lip, she'd experienced a pleasure above and beyond that of kissing. While kissing, there'd been a sum of uncertainties that the moisture of their mouths glued together hadn't resolved. The punch, on the other hand, had established a certainty: in life – at least in hers – it was better to be able to fight than to get flustered with tongue action.

Coming back home that day, she'd found her mother on the sofa, watching a rerun of *Beverly Hills, 90210*. America, always, whatever the era.

"You've torn your T-shirt? You think clothes grow on trees?"

Vanda had smiled. She didn't expect gratitude. Her torn T-shirt was her trophy, and her mother's telling-off underlined the power of her sacrifice. When you're nine years old, that's as significant as victory itself. She even ate her snack while watching Brenda arguing with her friend Kelly, totally serene.

There were some nice guys among her mother's lovers. Some developed a soft spot for her. She even remembers a small, dark-haired man she found very handsome – he looked a bit like Dustin Hoffman – who played with her, made up stories and put on different voices to animate her figurines. He gave her a box of Indian dolls and a little plastic horse with the mark of a red hand on its rump. There were also some arseholes, it's not like her mother had any talent for clever observation or only made wise choices. Most of the time, she thought with her pussy and – something Vanda realized later – she didn't want guys who were too good for her, who could judge her – and on that front she showed a great deal of common sense to avoid pain and guilt. They weren't supermen but not monsters either. Some may even have possibly wanted to stick around, but her mother got bored quickly, unless it was that she didn't want to tie herself down to a man, so a matter of choice. Vanda isn't necessarily able to analyse this – in any case it's obvious that back then she wasn't in a position to draw any insightful conclusion about their lives. Sometimes, she's like her, and finds that very possibility unbearable. It's good to live far away from her.

The first time Vanda caught her mother in a lively doggy-style act, it was with him, Dustin Hoffman. She had been dragged out of bed by thirst and the two bodies were wriggling on the living-room sofa, the scene lit up by the glow from the television screen, *Jaws* accompanying her mother's hip movements, the clenching of the guy's white buttocks. Quickly losing interest in the two agitated bodies that slotted into each other passionately, her attention was caught by the giant fish on the screen, eating chunks of the *Orca*, the struggling little boat. The guys were in big trouble, their boat was taking in water and listing dangerously, the monster wouldn't die despite the harpooning and the yellow cans attached to its back. It was fascinating.

If her mother hadn't screamed, noticing her standing still a metre away from the sofa, Vanda would have continued watching the film. Naked and enraged, she yelled at her daughter, screaming loud to cover up her own embarrassment, and sent her back to bed. Afterwards, Dustin Hoffman disappeared. Pity, because she quite liked him. Eventually, she did catch her mother with a man on other occasions, or needed to push her earphones deep into her ears so she wouldn't hear her.

Once, just once, her mother struck gold, a real arsehole, he slapped Vanda because she'd made fun of his shoes. He didn't last long. For all her casualness, her mother didn't wish her daughter any harm and threw the man out of their home with liberal lashings of serious and legal threats.

"My mother fucks whoever she likes, even your father if she fancies it."

The blond boy had attacked her, but in the end she'd been the one to make his nose and gums bleed. It didn't take long to set Vanda off. But, deep down, there was the pain of humiliation, her mother called a whore – in secret after that. In this Breton village Sundays were still filled with church: having a kid without a father, not being married and being comfortable with a voracious sex appeal made people talkative and nasty. The mother knew what they were saying in the village, but she never suspected that her daughter also had to pay the price. Vanda grew up, learned to shave her legs after the unpleasantness at the pool, never cut her hair, which cascaded down her back in fat curls, like a provocation. All the guys fantasized about grabbing them in handfuls to guide her face – what with her mother's baggage, you could say it was inevitable the little hooligans should dream. And that's all they did, since she had a very hard fist and a shitty temper. Vanda hated everybody, has never set foot there since she left. In the beginning, she called her mother every so often, then increasingly seldom, then she stopped. Her mother was always complaining, and then reproachful. She doesn't even know she's a grandmother.

Vanda also remembers a teacher, from Mali, when she was in middle school. He must have been the only black man in the village and he was painfully aware of it. The level of racism was proportionate to the coarse ignorance that prompted the insults. He persisted for a year before he finally snapped and left for Rennes. He taught maths and she'd draw during his classes. The day he noticed, Vanda prepared herself for a telling-off. He kept her back after the bell, when everybody else ran out yelling. She waited, standing by his desk, as he examined one of her drawings. He took ages, then finally sighed.

"It's too small for you here, Vanda. You must leave when you're older. Don't stay here."

And she thought exactly the same, so much so that a wave of warmth and gratitude drifted through her, from her pubis to her neck. He gathered the drawings to give them back to her, having put one aside – a bush which, depending on the angle at which you looked at it, had a face.

"I'm keeping this one. War booty. All right?"

While nodding energetically, she happily left her sketch to the weary teacher. As for maths, it wasn't even mentioned. She thought how she'd have liked for this one to be her mother's lover. After the holidays, he'd already left and she never saw him again.

Vanda opens her eyes. This morning, the light enters in rays, with dust dancing between them. The goldfinch is singing gently, she likes that. On the other hand, its cage stinks, she must change the newspaper at the bottom. And she must remember to take it out more often, it's not made for living in the dark. Since the aborted meal on the cliff road, surges of anxiety have been waking her up every morning, she has dreadful nightmares – death prowls and tears her or Noé to shreds, in great scenes of carnage. Last night didn't escape the rule. Simon hasn't given any sign of life yet, but she has a strong feeling the game isn't over: she's still on alert and checks her mobile a bit too often. She lights a joint stub lying in the ashtray by the bed. She should bare her teeth again. Make gums bleed. Or learn to dodge the blows.

Noé is wrapped in his duvet, his sleeping face turned towards the bird. It's dizzying, watching him sleep – his breathing, his relaxed body and this inner life that revolves in his slumber. When she watches him sleep, the end of the world gets close, in a blend of fear and fatalism. To ward it off, Vanda takes off her clothes, slips on the one-piece Lycra swimsuit with straps that snap on her skin when she puts them over her shoulders. Her body is hard, her flesh taut and soft. The patterns are a part of her, her body is fertile ground for the flowers blooming and twining around her. When there are men on the beach, they watch her going in or out of the water with the gormless expression of Greek peasants discovering Aphrodite bathing. Softly, taking care not to wake Noé, she leaves the hut and pops out into the light. She doesn't feel cold – maybe it's the joint or else the feeling of strength that the desire to swim gives her – and runs at full speed until she's slowed down by the weight of the water against her legs. Then she dives.

You Don't Always Get to Do What You Want

She suspected as much, of course. The head of department had warned her. The HR woman's waited for her to finish her working day before she summons her. The worst thing is that she doesn't even mention her lateness or her strike-related absences. The conclusions of the administrative takeover were irrevocable, and the HR manager explains it with the commiserating expression of subordinates who don't have a choice.

"We have to cut down on staff."

"So I'm sacked, am I?"

"Your contract won't be renewed, so it's not exactly the same thing."

"In practice, it's the same thing for me."

The HR manager sighs. She can't afford to be too understanding, otherwise people walk all over you. Vanda says nothing, stares at the desk, the papers cluttering it, the desktop background with a Texan landscape or Death Valley, or some other canyon like that. Orange exposure, setting sun.

"Shall I leave now?"

"No, you're contracted to work till the end of the month, so we're counting on you."

There's a hint of anxiety in the HR manager's voice – the bitch isn't going to let them down now, they still need her.

"Why me?"

"You're not the only one, rest assured."

"I don't find that reassuring."

Silence takes root. The HR manager rolls her pencil between her fingers, tries to signal with a smile that the meeting's over.

"I need this job."

"Like everybody else, but you don't always get to do what you want."

"I don't understand."

"What don't you understand?"

"I thought we were short-staffed."

The HR manager opens her mouth to answer but seems to swallow her words instead. She hesitates, looks at Vanda.

"That's two different things."

Vanda thinks that they're above all two contradictory things, a bit like cutting the number of teachers to promote education or abolish benefits to fight poverty. She's not impressed by that kind of illogicality. At the pace at which nonsense multiplies, psychiatric hospitals are going to get more and more crowded, that's so obvious you don't need a degree in political science to work it out. It could drive her round the bend, and others with her. The throbbing in her temples puts pressure on her head. To say that she wants to knock over the desk in front of her would be euphemistic.

When she leaves, the head of department calls her and takes her arm, explains she doesn't have the authority to make decisions, if that were the case she'd keep Vanda, she's a hard worker and gets on well with the patients. She's frowning, her eyes are tired. Vanda saw her at the demonstration, shouting with the others. She's holding the newspaper, opens it with a regretful expression and shows her the front page: Vanda is easily recognizable, her long hair suspended, frozen in motion, her face angry in the middle of a tear gas cloud, panic around her. You can see a riot policeman, baton extended, a body on the ground. Vanda looks back up at the head of department, gestures at the HR office.

"Did she see it?"

"Yes."

"Is that why she's sacked me?"

"No, there really is a drastic cut in personnel, but let's just say this sped things up."

Vanda shakes her head, focuses on the picture again. She revisits the horror of the ultra-violent crowd break-up, the blows, the bleeding woman. She wonders if she'll dare to go on a demo again without kitting herself out as if for a war. If she'll have that kind of courage.

For the time being, in the face of the regretful supervisor and the end of her contract, Vanda feels rather dispensable, collateral damage. Too distressed to be a warrior. She leaves the hospital the way you run away, doesn't look out for Samia, who will no doubt be in the next round of redundancies. Outside, the bushes are already crackling in the heat – she runs to catch the bus, in her chest tremors like sobs, which she disguises as panting.

You Piss Me Off, the Lot of You

"Noé, you're going too fast."

"But we're really late!"

The get-together for Dimitri's birthday is at Parc Borély and Vanda is already dreading the thought of meeting the other parents.

"We're not late, we can go when we like, it's what the invite says."

"Didn't Dimitri's mum say three o'clock?"

"Yes, but people can turn up whenever they like after that. Do you really want to go?"

Concerned, Vanda bends over her son. Just to make absolutely sure that Noé is desperate to go chasing after coypus with his little classmates, because if it was just up to her, they'd go to the racecourse next door instead.

There's a large lake in the park, seldom more than fifty centimetres deep. It swarms with coypus that are so used to being fed by children that they're fat as pigs. You can't get too close, because they're still aggressive, their long, orange incisors ready to crunch kids' hands. A dirty breed with rat tails that pass themselves off as cute beavers. Vanda prefers the horses with the colourful silks. There's also a rose garden with flowers that wither as soon as the first days of intense heat arrive, and struggle to grow in the gusts of wind.

Much as Vanda adores being with her son and his solitary games, spending the afternoon with six other children and their parents feels like a punishment. She doesn't like to see him living outside their bubble, but she's not able to estimate the consequences of that.

They spot the right place because the birthday area is decorated with balloons attached to trees, and a cake buffet has been set up on the grass. Noé is waving to his friends. The parents turn their heads towards them and welcome Noé with an abundance of sweet words Vanda finds stupid and patronizing, because they don't come from her. She smiles anyway, says hello to everybody without taking physical risks – shaking hands in this kind of situation is ridiculous, kissing on the cheek is an ordeal. She fiddles with the small package for Dimitri, looks at Noé, who hesitates, goes back to her as he feels she needs him.

"You can go if you like, Maman, and come and pick me up at the end."

Vanda thinks that the sea is very close, that there's a park café where she'd like to sit away from the screaming, watch the lake turtles emerge with their prehistoric heads then plunge back into the mud. Dimitri's mother approaches.

"The mums can stay if they like, watching them enjoying themselves is so amazing, you never tire of it. But of course if you have to work, we'll gladly look after Noé. We'll be leaving the park by six."

"I'm not working today, but I wouldn't mind having a flutter on the races."

Dimitri's mum looks as if she's just crunched into an onion. Vanda feels so alone and cornered. She wanted to keep shtum but it just came out. Shit, it's the truth. The wrapping paper has got damp, fragile after all the kneading. Perhaps to compensate for her unacceptable desire to run away, she holds out the present, stuffs it into the hands of the tall brunette with straight hair in an inverted bob.

"It's for Dimitri. Noé chose it."

"No point in staying, if you don't like spending time with children."

Oh, so it's clear and to the point – Dimitri's mother doesn't go for the polite smile or selective deafness. She replies like an empress, filled with the certainty that she's on the right side, on the side of comfortable choices and total commitment. She knows what's good for children, she cooks organic vegetables, reads her son stories every night. Intelligent, subtly educational stories, never Disney. She rolls her eyes when Dimitri asks for a ham-and-cheese escalope, like in the canteen, gets offended when she discovers that he knows things – words, films, characters – he certainly didn't learn about at home and that she never wants to hear about again, is that clear? In a way, she's already triumphant, her son's been on the winning side from the start. Such comfort, such satisfaction. The fight isn't even a real fight, their right-mindedness acts as truth. The other parents are listening, even if they pretend they're not. Vanda feels she's being told off like a little girl. She remembers the HR bitch, spinning her pencil, dismissing her with a glance at the door. Simon, who thinks he knows better than her. Everyone seems to think they know better than she does, fuck them all.

"You piss me off, the lot of you."

"Excuse me?"

The brunette freezes, not at all prepared for this kind of response. In her world, people are polite. They love children and would do anything to make them happy, even at the cost of sacrifices they'll make sure they won't reproach them for. They have jobs they enjoy, fulfilling if not lucrative. They attend school board meetings, their parenthood, like a flag, proudly pinned to their Fairtrade jackets. They sometimes drink a bit too much, but never so much they can't remember anything the next day. They're moderate because they're grown up. A life Vanda doesn't want but also thinks she'd like to have. The complexes, the disdain.

"I'm sorry, I'm taking it out on you because of other people. I'm tired."

Her fingers on her temples, Vanda attempts a faint smile. She doesn't want Noé to be given dirty looks because of her.

"It happens to us all."

Vanda doubts they could possibly mean the same thing, but says nothing.

"Noé, go play with your friends."

But Noé doesn't move, hanging on the exchange. Thimothée's father chooses this moment to appear with a cake in his hands, a saviour.

"I recognize you," he exclaims, smiling at Vanda. "You were on the front cover of *La Marseillaise* last week, weren't you?"

Vanda no longer knows if the ground is hostile, the guy's smile just told her it isn't, so she nods.

"Were you there, too?"

"At the protest? Yes, but at the tail end of the procession. We got hit by tear gas but managed to run towards Les Réformés."

Dimitri's mother looks surprised, but the fact that Vanda was at the demonstration almost makes her less hostile than earlier. Joint struggle, Vanda thinks ironically, doubting very much that their fights could possibly be compatible.

"I saw a woman with a cracked skull and the police kept hitting her."

"It was awful. I'd never seen anything like it."

Noé relaxes. He doesn't care what the adults are saying, as long as his mother is neither sad nor angry, and especially not because of him. He comes up to her, pulls her arm to speak into her ear, cups his hands around his mouth and whispers, "I love you."

This trickles into Vanda's belly, it's as if everything is being put back in its place, from organs out of alignment to blood blocked in her veins making her movements stiff. She replies, using the same system. "Me, too, my Limpet. Go play with your friends."

The child runs away to the lake shore: two coypus emerge and heave themselves up gingerly onto the bank, wet and inquisitive. The kids are revelling.

She ends up staying. It's not that she enjoys it, but she prefers to keep an eye on Dimitri's mother, in case she starts talking rubbish about her, with her son nearby. She serves out the slices of cake, chats a bit, but does a lot of dodging. She also watches Noé playing and taking his place at the heart of a group of children – this part of him escapes her and that's painful. The other parents are friendly, talk to her, she's bored shitless. Moreover, Thimothée's father hasn't stayed.

At some point she listens carefully so she can hear what the kids are saying, that's what she finds interesting. A little girl says she went on a rowing boat on the lake with her aunt. A child replies that, well, his father took him for a ride on a motorbike.

"My father has a scooter, too!" Noé cries.

Something tears through Vanda's stomach. Her head is buzzing, heavy and electrified. Like when she goes to bed too drunk and her head plunges too far down in an endless fall that makes her want to throw up. Nearby, the other parents haven't heard, haven't paid attention. She can picture them grimacing with satisfaction, talking to Simon and telling him how pleased they are to have a conversation with him, it was a real disaster with the mother, so aggressive and couldn't even bake a cake for a birthday. From that moment on, she isn't really there any more. She wants to run away, climb a century-old tree and remain perched up there so no one sees her, or go back to their hut, take Noé in her arms and never let him go. His lock flies as he makes a football pass, his face lit up, not thinking to look at his mother.

"I'm going to take a walk to the lake," she tells Dimitri's mother, trying to conceal her distress and smooth over the violence of their previous exchange in an appeased tone. "Will you keep an eye on Noé?"

"Of course," the mother replies, as soft as a cashmere cardigan.

*

When they get home, later, Vanda's bag crammed with cake leftovers, handfuls of sweets in Noé's pockets, the child will tell with his arms, in a voice more excited than usual, about his day's victories – in football and in making a twig dam in the mud. Haunted by his future, desirable, flying the nest, Vanda won't be listening. One day, he'll grow up and she'll be alone. One day, he'll overwhelm her with his large body and she won't be able to protect him with her two arms. His soft, small hands will no longer slide on her palm, he'll go away. He'll love, suffer without her. On their way back, she'll resist the desire to stifle him in her arms a little, but not completely, will interrupt his babbling with a sudden hug, too solemn, to which the child will respond before escaping and running to the beach.

Carrion

When facing danger, there aren't countless options. If an attack is impossible and so is defence, all that's left is escape. This notion finds its way into Vanda's head. She thinks more clearly when she swims, so that's what she's been doing for at least half an hour. There's no school today, and no work either. She rang early this morning to say she wouldn't be going in, that her son was ill. In any case, at this stage, they can go fuck themselves.

As soon as she woke up, she sat on the edge of Noé's bed, dark rings under her eyes after a terrible night.

"You like Simon?" she asked.

The kid looked at her with his soft, large pupils still full of sleep, you could tell he was suddenly worried, that he didn't know what to answer. He dared a *yes*, shy and stammering, closely followed by a *don't know*. She sat there, on the same spot, bearing the brunt of it, elbows digging into her thighs. He reached out and touched his mother's shoulder, the magical, colourful halo of the fairy, traced her delicate features.

"Maman?"

Faced with his mother's immobility, Noé sat up in bed, put his arms around her neck, clung to her.

"Actually, I made a mistake, I don't like him."

"You're allowed to like him, Limpet," she said, still motionless. "We're OK, the two of us, right?"

"Yes."

"It's us two against the rest of the world."

She's gone swimming, leaving him in pyjamas in front of the computer, watching a cartoon with talking animals.

She's angry with him. Sometimes, she pictures him dying. Every situation pushed to an extreme of disaster, imagining the worst in order to avert it. This often leaves her distraught, shaking with anxiety.

She imbues every stroke with superstitious diligence. Like children who step on patterns on the ground, imagining traps and victories depending on a flawless route, she counts the seconds spent underwater, doesn't permit herself less than five, better if longer, but minds she doesn't get breathless, fewer than five would be the end of the world, fewer than five and the cliffs would tumble into the water and bury the beach, fewer than five and a Leviathan would swallow her whole.

So, it's escape. It's the solution that materializes in her head, and Tangier rises up from the waves, the white city of Tangier. She also remembers the slaughter of tuna, one day in the harbour. Tunas caught in fishermen's nets, harpooned from the boats, the red water – *we have to earn a living*, the fishermen sniggered among themselves when they saw her eyes wide with pity.

And then the shipyard, the bloated hulls, ribbed with salt. Boats out of the water, asking to return to it. Blue boats. Blue. Blue. The bellies of all the boats are blue, over there. And she remembers the chubby skeleton of that huge boat being built that reminded her of human bones. She doesn't know that the harbour has since been concreted over. She's not sure that life in Tangier would be easy for her, she's not sure it would be a permanent solution, but it's an El Dorado that would allow her to put some distance between her and everybody else, especially Simon. Find new solutions far away from everyone, fall off the radar. Protect her son. She has a memory of an easy life for foreigners, even broke ones. She thinks about Françoise and Joseph, about their kindness. Her memory is possibly embellishing, and the grandiose lights that come on in her skull may be just worn-out headlights. It's possible but it doesn't change anything. Besides, with Noé, she can do anything. No less than five seconds, a stroke slicing through the cold water, a one two three four five, jasmine blooming in corollas, one two three four five, the narrow streets in the medina, the smell of freshly baked bread, of strawberries. Françoise's smile.

When she surfaces, her vision's still blurred, but when she dives, the bottom's clear. A few drops have gone into her swimming goggles, in the corner of her eye, but she refuses to empty them – she'd break the magical rhythm, the five seconds it's necessary to hold her breath so her project's a success.

Through her goggles, she makes out a strange form by the shore and some swimmers calling out to one another, pointing with their fingers at a dark stain approaching in time with the backwash. The form seems inert but when the swimmers approach it, it seems to move slightly. Vanda dives towards the shore, holds her breath even longer to get there quicker, her entire body pushing against the current that's returning out to the sea, using the one that folds the water back towards the beach. As soon as she feels the sand under her outstretched toes, she snatches off her goggles, lets them hang like a necklace. Panting, she senses tragedy in the dying body of the cetacean. Three swimmers are as distressed as she is, stunned by seeing such an animal on one of their beaches – you only see them out at sea, not so close to the French coast. It looks like a very large dark dolphin with a beluga nose. It has trouble breathing, and even more swimming, despite the encouragement of the four humans panicking at the prospect of seeing it die before their eyes. Suddenly, a fifth voice joins the shouts, a small, desperate voice – it's Noé, he's come out of the hut, run down the beach and gone into the water in his pyjamas. He's stroking the smooth skin and the curved dorsal fin, asks the animal to rally its strength and swim back out to sea. Vanda doesn't yell at him, doesn't ask him to go back home. It's a huge animal, must weigh at least two tons, and it rolls onto its side. It's not a living movement but rather one of abandonment. Later, they will learn that it's a long-finned pilot whale that lives in a group from the age of ten to twenty, that it's a sociable animal with a life expectancy of sixty years. For now, all they see is an enormous creature in the process of dying, that's come to beach here, nose first. They can't manage to push it back into the water, especially as they all feel that they're going against its will, that the animal doesn't want to swim any more. Their arms are hurting, panic sweeps over them. One of the swimmers is shaken by a sob. "Damn it, fight!"

The others look up, their eyes meet. Noé's eyes don't leave the animal. His face is tense, focused. His hands are on the muzzle of the cetacean, already soiled with sand.

"It doesn't want to fight, it wants to die."

Vanda has to skirt around the enormous animal to reach her son and take him in her arms. One of the swimmers has gone up to his things to call for help – or the press? Who do you call when an animal commits suicide? Who do you inform when it's a whale, made for living in a pack in deep waters, come to die on a beach, alone?

"It's not the first," one of the swimmers says with sadness. "Three dolphins were beached on the Spanish coast. And in Greece. Near Nice, they managed to push a kind of whale back into the sea, but fishermen found it dead among the rocks the next day."

Vanda shudders and her shudder turns to trembling. Despite the sun and the absence of a strong wind, the cold creeps up on her in tremors. The animal must be five or six metres long, its tail is floating, stirred by the backwash.

"Why do they do that?" Noé asks, the bottom of his pyjamas floating around him, his hands still stroking the animal's head.

While the well-informed swimmer tells Noé about climate change, the melting ice caps, the migrations caused by humans and the seas full of plastic bags, Vanda feels the smell of the end of the world grab her like in the middle of a nightmare. She stupidly wonders if it's her fault, if she miscalculated, didn't hold her breath for that extra second. She pushes panic away by breathing deeply, in jolting gulps. She inhales as the cetacean exhales once and for all and discreetly, its tiny round eye on Noé. She'd like to go swimming again – it's a sudden, powerful urge, but she fights it in order to stay with her son, sucks her salty lips, wrinkled by the sea.

What the fuck's the point of eating organic or turning off the tap while brushing your teeth when it's already dead. When the dead bodies of animals come up all the way to your bikini. Soon, kids will lump them all together – unicorns and white tigers, sphinxes and aurochs. They – people – are also going to drop dead. She's keenly aware of that, like an animal about to be put down, and thinking that, when it happens, Noé might still be around, drives her insane.

"Are you all right, madame?"

Vanda shakes her head to say no, but contradicts herself with a smile.

"I've just called the police, they're informing the harbour. They're going to tow it into the sea so they can take care of it in a less public place."

"Take care of it?" Noé asks, filled with new hope.

"It's dead, so they have to... well..."

The man hesitates to explain the cutting-up process to the child. He's right. Noé's upset enough as it is, his brown eyes brimming with tears he's holding back out of reserve.

"They're going to cut it up, Limpet."

Surprised, the hesitating man stares at Vanda. He doesn't have children, tells himself she must know what she's doing, he wouldn't have dared, really, and now the kid's crying. His mother takes him by the hand, pulls him towards the hut. The wet cotton fabric sticks to his legs, making him look like a skinny bird. The man watches them disappear behind the chipped shutters.

Now that she's made up her mind, she'd better get on with it. Maybe it won't be any better in Tangier, but it's the perfect place to wait for the end of the world.

Healing Fingers

When Vanda goes to work today, no one knows it's her last day. She washes everything methodically, shines the sinks with strange energy. Cleanliness takes on a new meaning, she wipes away the grime with definitive gestures, wets the floors with floods of water, scrapes in order to create paths that are less sticky, less smelly.

She didn't use the money Simon gave her to fix her car, which is still asleep on the pavement, soon to be impounded. She spent the money on two airline tickets. And there's still a bit left over, Simon was generous. Impatience has been eating away at her for two weeks, because they had to wait for Noé's passport.

Although her decision has made her giddy, it's a euphoric, liberating giddiness. A leap into the void, but with wings. They're off. The day of their great departure, their bags will be light – the bulkiest thing is Noé's toys, he broke down at the prospect of abandoning them. She'll leave the stuff she doesn't absolutely need. In any case, she won't be paying the final rent instalment, so that's a saving, the landlord will be pissed off but he can always take whatever they'll have left behind. They're expected at their destination, Françoise couldn't believe it, her voice sounded older on the phone. She said Joseph had been ill but was better now, and yes, of course Vanda could come. They can stay for the first few weeks, then Françoise will help them find somewhere, because Joseph gets tired quickly now when there are guests. Vanda has planned everything, and will even ask Jimmy to drive them to the airport without telling him where they're going. He's bound to sulk, but he's zany enough himself to understand crazy decisions.

Vanda is tense, full of images, her throat vibrates with excitement whenever she feels the printed tickets under her smock, in the pocket of her tired parka – it'll soon be too warm to wear it anyway, and it'll be even worse over there. Silently, after doing her shift, she says goodbye to every patient, paying particular attention to each. She even accepts a cuddle and a trickle of saliva on the back of her smock from Jared. Then she decides to go and see Magalie, who doesn't want to leave her room.

Vanda watches her from the doorstep. Magalie doesn't even look at her, turns her back and stares at an invisible dot on the wall. Vanda puts a carton of cigarettes by the headboard, Marlboros without a death warning on the box, the kind you find under the table, at the flea market or in some abandoned districts in the city centre. Bits of contraband that arrive from Russia or elsewhere, so strong that one's worth two. Magalie still doesn't move, but Vanda knows she's paying attention to her every gesture despite her apparent apathy, and that she's seen the cigarettes. She blinks when Vanda takes from her bag a silk scarf she stole from Monoprix the day before. There's a tiny little tear where she removed the anti-theft device, but the scarf is shiny, all blue and flowery, soft under her fingers. She's glad at the thought of Magalie wearing the soft fabric around her neck, even over her pyjama top. She puts it down next to the carton and leaves.

In the corridors, she walks past a few nurses crumpled with impatience, closed off. The room of the patient who died last week is already occupied by another. The staff are still gloomy, damaged by his death, worried that it might start again. After visiting Magalie, Vanda goes to the tea room to see the women who've been working with her for two years or two months, depending on their contract. They're on a break, massaging their feet, their flesh that swells in their shoes by the end of the day, complaining and giggling, less and less, though, as their numbers drop over time. Some of them are still on strike, and will be fired as soon as they get back. Vanda won't wait for the end of the month. The temping agency will pay her for the days she worked. Then they'll find another woman to exploit, and quickly, too.

Samia is helping herself to coffee, gets a second cup for Vanda, puts both on the table, between the leftovers of an unfinished lunch, a mobile phone with a golden case and a box of pills. It's not for the patients but the Doliprane they hand one another to get through the day when it's thumping too hard in their exhausted heads.

"I can't take it any more," Samia says, flopping on a chair with a grimace of pain.

"Still your back?"

Samia nods, clenching her teeth. A blonde with dark rings under her eyes slides the sugar bowl towards her, a box of biscuits brought back from Normandy. On the back of the lid, there are half-timbered cottages as incongruous as UFOs for women here. Vanda is emotional about going, she didn't think she'd be affected by leaving this job, these people. She notices, surprised, that her colleagues have pinned the newspaper front page to the wall, in the entrance hall. It makes her smile in the middle of her anxiety. She's leaving a little mark here. She goes up to Samia, stands behind her and places her hands on her tired shoulders. She presses, massages, makes her thumbs roll gently on her shoulder blades. Samia groans, halfway between pain and relief.

"*Wallah*, it feels good. Honestly, Vanda, you have healing fingers. You could make some money with that."

The women joke, talk about the sister of a husband, who opened a salon, about a physio who's too rough and does more harm than good, pillows placed at the foot of the bed to raise your legs, so the blood circulates after hours on your feet. Samia's shoulders soften under Vanda's hands. She's a bit ashamed she hasn't told anybody she's leaving, but she doesn't have a choice. Nobody must suspect she's flying to Tangier soon, nobody. She ends up drinking her coffee, lukewarm and milky, smiling at the others, barely listening to their chatter about helpful tips, wishes for the weekend, the latest about this patient or that one. Some of them go back to work with a sigh, while others get ready to go home, like Vanda.

For this last time, she decides to kiss on the cheek the colleagues who are here; they're vaguely surprised by this – Vanda hasn't got them used to this kind of closeness.

Then she leaves, for the last time.

A Pleasant Farewell

No end of the world without revelry, no departure without a celebration, even if everything has to remain a secret.

She got the word out about this evening, a big barbecue on the beach, a party to start the summer, drinks and music. Come with your kids and your dogs, your playlists and your stuff for grilling, we'll dance and the neighbours in the real houses around won't say anything because they know it'll make it worse, a war of nerves that can last the entire spring. We'll invite them, to see what they do. Nobody must know that they're leaving in two days' time, it's a party but for her it's a leaving do.

There's music, beer, bonfires. Not big fires, so no one informs the police. A few other kids. Dogs the children play with, despite the jaws of some of the mastiffs. Vanda doesn't know everybody, even though most look familiar to her. She's bound to have come across them one day or night, no doubt sozzled, a long time ago or last week. It's a damaged little assortment, some from the other night and others, hangers-on – alcohol, music and a barbecue always work, and if you throw in the chance of a night-time swim, then people find a way of cramming into cars or taking a crowded bus with no ventilation, oily sardines in the chaos of the only road that leads to the cove.

She even told Simon, in case he wanted to come for a drink – a way of not raising the alarm, of showing her credentials before scampering off without looking back.

Chloé is with him, she took a few days off and the TGV. It's a reunion with hesitant discussions – she's accepted his need to spend some time here, even though it's beyond her. She's still tense, hopes it's just a crisis, the grief and all that. She's waiting. And if she has to go and drink beer on the beach and meet the kid to help Simon come through it, then fine. When she arrived at the apartment, though, she was a bit shocked by the bedroom transformed for Noé. She wondered where this child business would lead them. Simon has even done some work, built a wooden mezzanine in the small, bright, repainted room. Since she talked to her best friend, who told her she was exaggerating, Chloé has been trying to be more understanding and come up with solutions not for her but for them. She's not used to it and, up to now, Simon's wishes were twinned with hers, unless he was the one to drift along with hers, who knows, she'd rather not think along those lines. She quite likes to decide for the both of them, but if anyone points that out, she denies it with loud protestations.

As she steps onto the beach, Chloé is forced to admit that it looks stunning. An orange sun beginning its descent offers a striking picture. The gilded faces, the ginger shadows, red contours. Up close, everybody's eyes have a liquid depth, like Photoshopped reality. And then there's the sea, omnipresent, glimmering at this time, the backwash taking up a large part of the sound space.

As she approaches the hut, Chloé recognizes "London Calling", the wolf imitation that several guys, already topless, intone, laughing. Simon sees a friend in the middle of the group, a guy from art college he quite liked, introduces him to Chloé. This increases her sense of isolation.

As for him, he's been watching Noé for a while, has spotted him near the rocks, playing with a huge dog. He wishes he could shout to everyone that it's his son, but apart from the fact that it would make him look like a loony, it could frighten the child – and, he realizes, Chloé. He'd also quite like someone to be concerned that Noé's playing with an animal without a collar, that could crunch his face in a single snap of the jaws, so close to the rocks that he's certain to be ripped to shreds at the slightest fall. There's even a rusty old sign that forbids access to that part of the beach, heralding danger. Simon would rather he played with the other children, except that the other children are eating their sausage sandwiches, watched by adults who, even if they're party animals, are planning on retreating to the city centre by nightfall. He listens to this old friend telling him about his journey, the hell of being an artist, of living on peanuts. He listens with one ear, nods half-heartedly, looks for his son, doesn't understand how Vanda can be at once so protective and possessive with her child and yet leave him so totally unsupervised. And he suddenly wonders where Noé was the night he saw Vanda again. Simon realizes from the silence of the guy in front of him that he's just been asked a question. So he asks for more details to hide the fact he hasn't been listening to a thing, angry at seeing Vanda dancing, drunk already.

Her hair is dancing with her, it's a powerfully sensual asset, whether she likes it or not. The night is slowly falling, there are still colours at the far end of the sea, but it's growing darker around them and the wind has started blowing. On the other side, towards the city, the sky has taken on an opaque green colour, like the flesh of an aubergine. A colour Vanda adores, and which heralds a thunderstorm. They've got time until this green spreads to the coast. A friend sways towards Vanda and dances to a haphazard choreography. She has short hair and the face of a young girl, loose movements – her arms follow a rhythm that's independent from the rest of her body – but not muddled. The two dancing women attract looks. Around them, there are other dancers, laughter, groups sprinting on the sand to trip one another up, all so you can fall in a heap and feel others' heartbeat without the need to talk. The hut is kept shut, even more than usual: so no one sees their things stacked up, the rectangular, red-black-blue-striped bags, the two huge suitcases. She sometimes goes in alone to restock the gang with water for the pastis and ice cubes. The rest of the refreshments have been laid out outside the door on a beach towel. Everyone helps themselves.

People have eaten, crunched sand with bread, some left afterwards, especially those with children, or the few who have jobs. The rising wind is charging at the party guests, who have to shout louder, feel the backwash but can't see it since it's now night. You can guess the crest of the waves, the sluicing, tumbling whiteness. People feel like swimming, even more so now it's dark. They're going to swim naked or in their underwear, with that fear in their belly from being unable to see anything, the blackness below, the eddies they feel even more strongly and the current that could pull them into the open sea. It's for the frisson, since the spot isn't actually dangerous, but Vanda still has in her mind the span of the beached cetacean, imagines dark forms and sharks that have left the open sea to loiter by the coast. Even so, she removes her jeans, abandons them rolled up in the sand. Noé joins her. He wants to swim, she refuses. But the adults are doing it and the children have all gone. The kid is swaying from tiredness, he's held up only by the excitement, his nerves mobilized to hang in there longer. She says no, says he must go to bed, and yet doesn't take him to the hut, the door of which is still shut.

"I can put him to bed," Simon offers, suddenly next to them.

His voice is controlled to hide his concern – the dogs, the late hour, the couples getting excited so close to the child, these plastered adults who pay attention to nothing or no one.

"It's OK, I'll take care of him in a bit."

Simon expected a refusal and even the snapping tone. He looks at Vanda's bare legs, the stretch marks where her hips start, like the undulating patterns at the bottom of a swimming pool. He retreats but approaches Noé as soon as his mother moves away. She watches the two of them talk as she helps herself to another drink. The day after tomorrow they'll be far away, she might as well leave him a few more minutes – besides, a guy comes to drink with her, it's the waiter she quite likes from the gig bar, the one who gives her vodkas on the house. He puts a hand on her waist, practically on her bum, but not so much she feels like prey, and this sends a charge through her sex, her thighs, so she presses her buttocks against his stomach. The guy, delighted, starts nibbling at her neck, it's direct and without hesitation, they're going to heat up and the beach is theirs despite the wind and the impending thunderstorm. Noé's still with Simon, his Parisian girlfriend is pondering a bit further while drinking wine, her eyes on the black water. Vanda reckons she's easily got time and takes her partner behind the rocks. Her sex is already soaked, swollen by the dancing, the drink, the sight of couples embracing in the darkest corners. The guy's the same, he tears off his trousers and helps her take off her underwear without falling over. They keep their T-shirts on, press themselves against the rock, he's immediately inside her, it's quick and nice, explosive. It climbs in the crescendo of a fanfare and she comes before him, the echoes rise all over her when he comes in turn. It makes them laugh, this speed, just as well they rushed, given their state, a laugh of complicity and celebration, of playful familiarity. It's not the first time they've got off together at the end of an evening.

"One day, we should sleep together," he says, looking for his jeans in the sand.

She smiles and doesn't answer, her hand still pressed against her sex to make it last. It's a pleasant farewell, she thinks, to fuck among the rocks on a party night, with summer on the way, laughter still in her mouth from having come so quickly and so strongly, almost together. She quite likes this guy. Not so much she'll tell him where she's going, but enough for him to be a lovely memory.

Vanda isn't planning to come back. She ventures a lie that doesn't commit her to anything, and that she really means:

"Why not?"

He's got dressed again, kisses her on the neck and hands her underwear to her.

"I have to shoot off, it's really late and I start my shift very early tomorrow. Will you come by the bar?"

She says yes, she'd like to, not tomorrow, but soon.

They weren't secluded for very long, but Noé is already asleep, his head against Simon's shoulder. The thunder is rumbling, getting closer. There's still a handful of die-hards around Vanda, still drinking, slumped in the sand. The braziers are out and Simon's girlfriend looks exhausted, time to chuck them out. The others can sleep on the beach, she doesn't care. Armed with her secret, she feels generous and powerful, ready to face Simon's eyes and his judgement. But he says nothing, just gently unsticks Noé's head from his shoulder and makes him flop against a jacket.

"I was waiting for you to come back so we could go."

"Can I give you a piece of advice?"

"Go on, but I've got quite a few for you."

"I don't want yours, especially if you're about to preach to me, but hear mine: get your girlfriend pregnant if you're that obsessed. I'm sure you'll make a great dad, all responsible and level-headed."

It's always the same with her, he can't tell if it's a compliment or if she's taking the piss. In addition, he doesn't like her use of the future tense. Shit, he already is a dad. But he says nothing, oddly calm, apparently shaken by something Vanda can't put her finger on. He signals to Chloé and they leave quietly, uneven footsteps in the sand, steadier on the steps.

Vanda is obliged to wake Noé, who's got too heavy for her to carry him to bed. He whines softly, stumbles against her and lets himself be led and put to bed without protesting, as limp as when he has a fever. He lets himself be undressed, kissed. Half asleep again, he digs his hands under his mother's neck, but she prizes open his fingers that are clasping her hair in a return to early childhood, strokes his forehead and nearly falls over while bending down to kiss him one last time.

Now she's wondering if she should turf out the pals who are too drunk to leave, whom she has no wish to see outside their home when they wake up in the morning – the rain finally decides, falling in cool, dense curtains, chasing away the last party animals, who get up grumpily.

Vanda has one last cigarette as she watches the water flow in rivulets on the sand, waves at the drinkers who are running away, their jackets over their heads like ridiculous umbrellas. She'll sleep for a few hours and finish packing their bags tomorrow, she's much too drunk to do it now.

It's been a lovely evening, she thinks, a summer salute, a perfect farewell.

You Have to Decide What You Want

Simon's leg is twitching nervously under his chair, even though Chloé's hand on his knee is soothing. The council clerk gestures at him to approach, he rushes, he's been waiting for twenty minutes, it's not long but the being still, the patience, has taken a toll on him. Now, at last, they're going to listen to him, give him some answers. He's glad Chloé's with him, makes it look more solid, a proper couple, and it also means she's with him in this business, not just on the fringes of it, disapproving. The employee tells him that yes, of course, a late acknowledgement of paternity is possible.

"Only, you'll never have parental authority. For that you need the FCJ."

"The what?"

"Family Court Judge."

Chloé, her head screwed on, intrudes: "My parents know some very good lawyers if it's what you really want, it means you'll have the same rights as her, so if she really starts playing up…"

"What do mean, mademoiselle?" the clerk asks.

"Well, let's just say that the mother isn't exactly…" She grimaces but doesn't dare say more, relies on the guy's perception, it can't be the first time he's hearing this.

"You can report this kind of thing. And it can be included in your application for paternity."

"I didn't know I had a son," Simon blurts out, like an apology. "She hid it from me."

"Yes, it happens, you're not the first."

"So what can I do?"

"If you contest her way of bringing up the child, that can speed up your application."

Simon feels sick, his hands grip the counter. It's a painful decision.

"She has sex in front of my son, he falls asleep in the middle of the night, she's always late picking him up from school. She lives in a hovel, hangs around with alcoholics."

The clerk expresses neither encouragement nor empathy; he's doing his job, that's all. "The judge can entrust your son to child protection."

"And?"

"If you think that would be best. But there's a chance he'll be placed in a foster family, and then it will be harder for you to get him back. Especially since you did not acknowledge him when he was born."

"But I didn't know he'd been born!"

"I understand, monsieur. I'm just explaining, that's all. Can you imagine if we took on trust all the fathers who wake up six years after their child was born?"

The guy has a point, Simon definitely realizes it. He scratches his scalp frantically, massages the back of his neck, refraining from a tantrum. He plays his trump card, the trigger for his action. "She's planning to take him abroad. What are my options?"

The man looks sorry, he shakes his head. "Now that's… complicated. She has the right, monsieur. You can try to stop her, but she has the right."

Simon's got Noé's room ready, decided not to sell the apartment, to alternate living here and in Paris. Even though Chloé doesn't look convinced, let alone happy at the idea, he still hopes he'll persuade her to come. He adds up his savings, what his mother left him. A kind of balance sheet of his life he's been running through for weeks. He'll find work here – it's not certain, but he has talent on his side, and the cost of living in this city is so much lower than in other places. He's already thought of a few guys, not as crazy as the skint artists he used to know, friends of friends who moved here from the capital two or three years ago, who saw that this city had enormous potential. It's still a rough area, but it'll go up, like everywhere else in the country. He feels a tiny bit dirty for thinking this way. Perhaps he would have liked to talk about his plans to his mother, perhaps he wouldn't have them if she hadn't died. With all the speculating and tying himself in knots, Simon clings to Noé, a gift in the form of a future, Noé, who provides a kind of palpability, of materiality. Noé who, last night, said he and his mother were going far away and wouldn't be coming back, before falling asleep on his shoulder, like a kitten.

"Can't I inform the police?"

"You can. I'm not sure they'd do anything about it, unless she wants to take him to Syria."

Simon gives a sarcastic little snigger, but the clerk wasn't joking. Chloé has slightly retreated, he keeps needing to prompt her with his eyes before she looks concerned. It gives him a pang to the stomach. With a gesture he hopes is controlled and mature, he stuffs the acknowledgement leaflets into his bag, says he needs to think about it, *thank you, monsieur, I'll get back to you as soon as possible.* The guy has nothing to add, he's already greeting the next couple for a wedding date. They're young, with lots of teeth – Simon thinks the man looks like a sporty jerk, with his trainers and his crew cut. Above all, as he examines the couple, he has an impression of something totally clear-cut, as if their outline was sharply defined. He feels old, badly shaved and blurry. He takes Chloé out of the town hall, hands her helmet to her.

It's stopped raining. It's a blue day, with leftover moisture in the creases of the asphalt. Chloé purses her lips. She's waiting for something, a decision, an expression of will, she promised herself that she would let him follow his path. He shakes his head.

"I don't want to do this. I can't."

"You have to decide what you want, Simon. One minute she's a crazy woman who's going to traumatize her kid, and next minute you can't do this to her because, after all, poor thing."

She promised herself but she's cracking, she can't stand her boyfriend's dithering any more, that's a fact.

"Shit, it's not that simple. You sound like everything's easy, black and white, you just have to decide what you want and act accordingly."

"Well, actually… yes. I think you're a coward."

He looks at her like a rebuffed child.

"I'm scared of doing something stupid."

"Then let's get out of here."

"What do you mean?"

"Let's get out of here, end of story. You sell your fucking apartment and we leave this city."

"My fucking apartment?"

Chloé's face seems to crumble, she shakes her head. Her voice becomes hoarse, she's fighting against collapse.

"It always sounds like I'm saying awful things to you, but all I want is for us to go back to being as we were. You and me. We had plans, we had a good life. I was happy. I don't like this city, it's disgusting and nobody gives a damn about anything. Nothing works, there's no shame, no jobs, there are open-air rubbish bins and guys who speak loudly and check out your arse like in the fifties. And I have to come all the way here because you've got obsessed with a kid. Frankly, I find this fixation insane, seeing as you didn't even know he existed."

He should reassure her, but he can't – the crack becomes a ravine.

"He's my son."

"Just because seven years ago you screwed without a condom."

"But, fucking hell, he exists!"

Soon, there are tears in Chloé's eyes, there's a feeling of a crisis, of the end of things, of stupid clichés. The couple from earlier exit the town hall chuckling, brilliant, good time to bring it up again, Simon and Chloé could join forces to bust their kneecaps.

"I feel like I'm losing you."

"Not if we do things together. I'm not going to let her leave. Are you with me?"

There's already a gulf between them, but they cling to the notion they have of themselves, of the couple they used to be, handsome and without a care, certain that they were free.

Chloé puts her helmet on, a sign of agreement, I'll get on and you drive, I'll come with you even if you're incapable of making a real decision – let alone the one she'd like him to make. She climbs behind him on the scooter, which struggles to start, it got flooded last night. Everything takes in water here – despite the blue, she can't help generalizing or using symbols, she wants to go back to her home, their home. Simon takes the road to the beach. And she notices, bitterly, that Simon hasn't asked a single question about her since she arrived. The child has entirely taken her place, and she already hates him.

Goldfinch

Vanda's still asleep and everything's creaking. True, it's no longer raining, but the wind is still blowing, a whirling wind, a sea wind that attacks in gusts and makes one jump. Noé wakes up against his mother, right up against her. He sniffs bad breath, the kind adults have in the morning, especially after drinking, but it comforts him – perhaps he already shares her taste for smells, the sense of life even if it smells like death. Noé buries his nose in her hair. When she's asleep, she belongs only to him. In a gesture of aborted awakening, she puts her arm around him and holds him tight, her chin on his head. Her skin is moist, scalding. He guesses from her breathing that she's gone back to sleep. He listens to his goldfinch singing, feels Vanda's movements, her swelling ribcage, and even her heart. He waits.

It's almost noon by the time Vanda wakes up. Noé has left the bed to play quietly then make coffee. He hasn't spilled anything, proudly shows off a cup he brings his mother in two careful strides. Tomorrow, they'll be in the large medina apartment, she can't believe she's dared do this, it's a bit like when she left Brittany, except that she's not on her own. Return to the place where she felt him for the first time. The two of them in Tangier. Even the hangover can't mar her joy, even though everything's amplified, her senses intensified.

She starts her computer, sends an email to Françoise: she's going to help her find something for later, a job, an apartment just for the two of them, a school for Noé. She also writes a message to Jimmy, but deletes it, it's too early. She thinks of the last things to cram into the suitcases and her eyes land on the birdcage. Shit, the bird's never going to get through as hand luggage and would die in the hold, that's assuming animals are allowed there. They're probably not, or else she should have organized it much sooner and, in any case, no, no, it's a bird you're not allowed to sell or keep in a cage. That's the word that helps her explain to Noé why they can't take it with them.

"It's like it's in jail, Limpet."

"You didn't say that when you brought it here."

"No, but we can't take it with us, it'll die on the plane."

Noé's cheeks are quivering and he has the stubborn expression he has on difficult days. And yet the day started so well.

"It's my bird. I love it."

"If you love it, give it back its freedom. It'll make some friends, find a girlfriend and maybe even have a load of chicks just like it."

His face tense, Noé looks at the bird. He's put the cage on his bed, his nose at beak level. He slides his hand through the little wire door, touches the red head with his fingertip.

"He's going to be really happy, build a nest in the hills," she insists.

The little boy surrounds the bird with his hand, in a pincer grip. He's trying to find the right way to hold it and especially not to let it escape in the room – it would bump against the walls – but is equally careful not to crush it. The goldfinch pecks at the boy's skin, isn't singing any more. It turns its head in all directions, its tiny talons tickling the child's fingers. Vanda sees that Noé is ready, so she walks ahead and opens wide the door of the hut.

Facing the sea, the child opens his fingers and the goldfinch takes flight clumsily but fast, quickly lands on the ground, takes off again, perches on the roof of the hut. It dares a few trills, inaudible because of the wind and the breaking waves, launches itself again, higher, flaps its wings to find its balance. A huge seagull nosedives, beak open, and swallows it.

Noé's scream is brief, devastating with surprise and despair.

He's My Son

From the top of the steps, Simon looks down at the beach. His eyes drift to the open doors of the shelter, the fresh paint of an outrageous Greek blue. The seagulls are flying low, turning in circles, nosediving into the waves. Chloé tightens her scarf even though the air is mild.

"Are you sure it's what you want?"

"There's no other solution."

"You could let go."

"And let my son go abroad with her?"

"Why not?"

"You saw how fucking unreliable she is, didn't you?"

Chloé sighs, pushes her fists deeper into the pockets of her jeans. This thing has been beyond her from the start. She wishes Simon hadn't known anything about this child, she didn't really want all this commotion. A gap in the kid's life, that wouldn't have been the end of the world. Simon experienced it himself and didn't make a big deal out of it.

"It's not like she's a monster, either. You want to be a father, OK, but you've only just appeared in his life."

In the end, she's the one who goes down first. Not to see Vanda and Noé, who are looking at the horizon in a daze, but to get closer to the sea. She's going back to Paris in two days' time, so might as well take advantage. At the water's edge, there are pebbles covered by the waves, you have to go up a little further to find sand.

Vanda sees them approach on the beach. She holds Noé against her, he's been silent since his goldfinch died at lightning speed. Vanda sulks, addresses only Simon.

"Fuck it, are you still here? Seriously, it's too much now. It's even freaky."

Simon faces her, sure of himself, feverish inside, a hand in the pocket of his jacket – he's rolling in his fingers the little green pebble Noé gave him.

"I want to see Noé and for him to come to my apartment."

"We don't need you, we've been managing very well for six years! I'm sick of you."

"By living in a hole? By not even being capable of picking him up from school? By drinking and fucking your mates instead of looking after him? You're a nutcase, Vanda!"

The certainty of his legitimacy is already less tremulous, more solid in his voice.

Vanda breaks down, crushed by the accusation.

"It's none of your business, you hear?"

"He's my son."

"Leave us alone! For fuck's sake, leave us alone!"

"He's my son!"

"Stop repeating that like an idiot. You've no business here."

"I have every right!"

Rage on both sides. She sees him grow in stature, strength and will. She wants to destroy him, for him never to have existed. Noé doesn't need him, they're going away. Tangier, Tangier. The word echoes inside her, she lets it flow in her mouth, between the bile and the terrifying dryness that overwhelms her. Tangier, the square with the cannons, the old theatre eaten away by the ivy, its gardens with the giant cacti, the bright pink of bougainvillea, the pale pink of the flowering laurels. Tangier!

"I know you want to leave with him, I won't let you."

The astonishment, the blow that cuts her in half, hits at her stomach. He can't know, no one knows. Except Noé.

She looks at the kid, who is now sobbing, snot on his lips. Little whimpers, shoulders jolting. His hair covers his temples, curls with sweat. He reaches towards her with one arm.

"I'm sorry, Maman, I'm sorry."

Her mouth part-open, she gulps the air as if she's just run several kilometres. She pulls him towards her, won't let go. And yet she wants to slap him, scream at him that it was a secret, a fucking secret, between her and him. She feels betrayed, but embracing him gives her the strength to turn to Simon again. She gives a fake smile, looks for a way out, her heart pounding, her throat crushed with fear.

"On holiday, we're going on holiday this summer. I can't see the problem."

"Stop it, Vanda, that's bullshit, don't take me for an idiot. In any case, I've informed the police and social services."

She's out of words, she's dying in the sand, the whole of her. Her face splashed with stupor, lips trembling. Also, her hands, which tense around the back of the child's neck. She glares at Simon with all the hardness she can still muster.

"Shit, why did you do that?"

"Because he's my son."

A moan of rage rises in her throat, and she exhales it with a grimace. She's ugly in her hatred. With her unruly hair, she's a gorgon rising before him. And yet he's not afraid. Rather, he feels he's winning the game.

She closes her eyes, holds Noé tighter, whispers *Why did you tell him, Limpet? Why?*

The white roofs, the terraces, the smell of grilled onion. The Rif cinema, the Grand Socco, the Sidi Kacem and Jbila beaches. She's pictured herself there with Noé a thousand times, the local or the French school, she wouldn't be late at leaving time. She would also have learned the language. Two immigrants, two travellers. She and her son. Of course, she's thinking about *Gloria*. Like the reel of a film that catches fire and melts at full speed, her El Dorado explodes, its beauty swept away. Powerlessness devours her whole, and anger with it. A demented ferocity flows through her, a ship lost in a storm, failure incarnate. She pushes Noé away, grabs one of the planks still lying around at the foot of the hut, one of the ones she couldn't face carrying up to the bins. She hurls herself at Simon, trips in the sand and the plank hits his knee.

"You're insane, that hurt!"

He rubs his knee, crouching, watches her grip her plank with the expression of a madwoman. He could place a hand on her shoulder, tell her they'll work it out. He could retreat, come back another time, later. Turn to

Chloé, who's waiting for him, draw some calm and reason from her weariness. But instead, he starts laughing, a victor's laugh. A laugh of humiliation, the laugh of the weak who are suddenly the stronger ones. He isn't even looking at her any more, but at the child, who's stopped crying but is standing there, frozen, holding the cuddly triceratops tight in his arms.

"Come, Noé, let's go. We'll be back to see your mother later. I want you to see your room."

Then, with a jolt, Vanda finds the strength to lift the plank with difficulty and sweeps the air with it until she hits the side of Simon's head. The blow is very hard but shouldn't have knocked him out. Only he collapses and doesn't move any more. For a few seconds, all you can hear is the relentless sound of the backwash, the shrillness of the gulls. Then Chloé's scream drowns out that of the birds and she runs to Simon, Simon's body, trips in the sand, gets back up, falls on her knees, doesn't understand why his eyes are open, why he's not moving any more. Only afterwards does she see the nail, the huge rusty nail rammed into his temple.

Vanda realizes at the same time. She turns away and rushes to Noé, grabs his hand, drags him into their shelter and shuts the door behind them.

Chloé can't scream even though that's exactly what she wants to do. Like in dreams when a faint voice escapes as the danger increases, she emits pathetic, breathless little cries. Terrified, she doesn't dare touch Simon, crawls backwards, her eyes crazy, darting from the body to the hut door, as if Vanda is going to come back out and finish her off, too. She takes out her mobile to call for help, decides to start running, holding her phone. The sand, the stone steps, they're steep but she climbs at full speed, runs back up the deserted bay, leans against a car and calls the police. Her throat sore, wheezing, she struggles to explain where she is, this fucking city is alien to her, she knows neither the street names nor the districts, and she's in shock. *Calm down, madame*, the police urge her, *tell us what you see around you.* Her eyes catch sight of a blue plaque, the name of a street, they know now, they're on their way. Then she lets herself slide down on the pavement, shaken by violent shivers.

Noé

When he suckled, small drops of sweat beaded his head, making his head damp and Vanda's arms damp. He'd lay his tiny hand on her breast, as a caress or a support. At times he'd squeeze the skin to bring out the milk. Sometimes, when full, he'd close his eyes, other times he watched her, measuring the world with his yardstick. When he bit her breast and she got angry, Noé would smile by way of apology. He'd press his nostrils against his mother's skin to breathe her in, even if that meant breathing in less air. When he woke up from his afternoon nap, she'd sing him "Funnel of Love".

Sometimes, she cried with rage at being unable to leave him there, and go walking, swimming, get drunk in the nearest bar. She shook with dizziness and power-lessness faced with this new appendage to her body. But she couldn't bear for anyone else to touch him. One day, when she had a cold, a woman in the metro gave her a tissue and patted the child's head with a tender expression, and Vanda imagined pushing her onto the rails. And yet she managed to leave him at the crèche, and happily at that – finally a separation from him, going back to work, and when she fetched him he had that heavy smell on his head, the smell of one of the crèche assistants, she knew which one, a smiling Comorian who spared no praise or gentleness. Vanda would give him a bath when they were home, removing the other woman's smell. Sometimes, she didn't have time, and then the scent smelled of betrayal. And then, later, school.

She spent many nights watching him in his sleep, his body tensing and then the surrender, the flabbiness of his cheeks, his half-open mouth. His way of curling up against her as he slept, before she had him sleep in his own bed. The questions, the fear of doing the wrong thing, the desire to run away, disappear, the evenings when she had him sleep in the back of the car so she wouldn't leave him alone. Her fits of anger when she wishes she were alone, her anxieties when she is.

At first, Vanda dragged their bags outside the hut, inebriated with a final hope of escape. Meticulously, with focused rage, she stacked up their things and urged Noé to help her. She kept repeating *Tangier, Tangier, Tangier,* listing solutions as non sequiturs. Falling apart a little more at each impasse. And then, suddenly, she remembered her car wouldn't start, that Jimmy would be asleep, that he owed her nothing and wouldn't get here fast enough, that the police would catch up with them. Simon was still lying in the same spot, looking as if he were resting on the beach, fully dressed. Chloé had disappeared, having run to take refuge in a little street at the top of the steps, frantically calling the police on her mobile, her hands agitated, her voice shrill. So, having taken everything into account, Vanda stopped walking, dropped the last bag in the sand. She looked intensely at Noé: there was a severe pain escaping from everywhere inside her, coming out of her eyes, irradiating the lines of her tattoos. A severe pain or something worse. Noé thought about the large cetacean who'd come to die on the shore.

They walked as far as the cliffs that emerge on the fringes of the beach, without rushing. They held hands, her skin was dry, she gripped Noé's fingers gently. He clung to her at every clumsy step in the sand. Vanda sat down facing the sea and Noé came to huddle against her, his back to her stomach. She embraced him, her body at one with his, from the chest to the ends of her arms.

The child strokes the knotwork of hair on his mother's neck, presses his nose to her dark skin, right on the poppy under her ear. Noé's heart is quivering on the brink of a sob, but the fear is too great to let out new tears. It's too soon. Perhaps the only defence is flight, a flying laugh that doesn't stem from anything funny, a laugh for its own sake, a laugh that hears itself shivering, rasping, beating the sound of the waves. A laugh that doesn't admit distance. The same laugh as his mother's.

He's six years old, he's about to lose everything.

The police arrive before the fire brigade, not that the firefighters have much to do, since Simon died on the spot, and there's no hope of resuscitation. Chloé can scream and beg, it won't change anything.

With a glance around, the police first discover Simon's body, as Chloé told them; she's now sitting fifty metres higher up, in a blue-white-red car, in a state of shock. She keeps repeating to herself that her final words to him were reproaches. She can't cry yet, she wants to go home.

Three men in uniform approach Simon's body and crouch. The nail sank deeply as if into butter and the plank is still covering part of his face. One of the policemen bends down to check: it was quick and practically painless, they'll remember to say this to his girlfriend later – survivors care about this kind of detail. But, for the time being, they have to deal with the rest – they look up and search the horizon, sweep the cove with their eyes, glimpse Vanda and her son, two silhouettes that make one. They're rocking in an embrace, looking at the sea. The little boy looks like he's laughing, so much so that the police wonder if those two are just ramblers who haven't seen anything of the event. But Chloé has given them a description of Vanda, her crazy hair, her tattoos, you couldn't really make a mistake.

The first policeman approaches, a hand on his holster. He has trouble walking on the sand, his gait is stiff and nervous and he takes absolutely ages to reach Vanda and Noé. He halts a few metres away, his voice isn't very confident – because of the kid next to his mother. He orders Vanda to place her hands on her head. She holds Noé close to her, you'd think she hasn't heard anything, except that there was a shudder, a shiver down her spine. and her arms locked tighter around Noé. The policeman has to repeat it in a graver, louder voice before she slowly obeys, her movements like a dancer at the end of a ballet. The policeman sighs with relief, comes closer to grab her wrists, handcuff her roughly behind her back. She still hasn't turned around.

"Step away, little one."

Another policeman has caught up with his colleague. They exchange two words, a sorrowful look, the policeman slowly approaches Noé – you'd think he was trying to catch a cat, even though the kid hasn't stirred. The first policeman takes Vanda away, he pushes her in the back to make her walk on the sand.

The other one chooses to sit next to the child. Noé is motionless, indifferent. His triceratops, neck squeezed in his fist, hangs his head limply against his cheek. A thumb in his mouth, index finger along his nose.

The man starts speaking to him gently, but it's complicated, he reaches out to the kid with one arm and strokes a lock of his hair without triggering the slightest reaction, then, when he tries again, the child pulls his head into his shoulders to dodge the caress. It's not clear what he's telling him, but it's easy to guess, or even picture the delicate paths he's obliged to take, the pregnant silences. It's easy to imagine he's upset, wants to take the child in his arms.

Behind them, Vanda has gone past Simon's body and is walking up the steps, now framed by four men.

Noé finally turns to the man who's speaking to him. He hasn't been listening to anything he's told him so far, hears only the modulation of the voice. He barely looks at him – the man tries to smile, his face crumpled.

"Do you have any questions now?"

The child slowly takes his thumb out of his mouth and wipes it on the triceratops's back. But he keeps silent. His large, brown eyes obstinately follow the flight of the seagulls. Perhaps he wonders which of them, in the flock, ate his bird.

As though motivated by the same decision, Vanda doesn't look at her son, who's still sitting, listless, facing the sea, and didn't turn around to see her leave either. It's as though they realized it was better to avoid it. Maybe Vanda warned him, asked him, *Don't look, Limpet, and above all don't turn around, just keep staring at the sea, only the sea.*

You and me, and the blue. You and me against the rest of the world.

Acknowledgements

Thanks to Clémentine Thiebault and Caroline Ripoll. They know very well what for, both of them.